LOVE RELEASED

WOMEN *of* COURAGE

EPISODE

7.5

NYT & USA TODAY BESTSELLING AUTHOR

GERI FOSTER

Love Released, Women of Courage: Episode 7.5
By Geri Foster

First Edition

Copyright 2015 by Geri Foster

ISBN-13: 978-1518854422

ISBN-10: 1518854427

Cover Graphics
Kim Killion
Lilburn Smith

Formatting: Dallas Hodge, Everything But The Book, www.ebeetbee.com

Author contact information: geri.foster@att.net

This is a work of fiction. Names, characters, places, and incidents are either the product of the author's imagination or are used fictitiously. Any resemblance to actual persons living or dead, businesses, events, or locales is purely coincidental.

DEDICATION

Dear Reader,

Thank you for reading Episode 7.5 of Women of Courage, Love Released. I know venues are filled with many authors and books and the choices are limitless. I'm flattered that you chose my book. There are additional books in this series and if you enjoyed Cora and Virgil's journey, I hope you'll read the others.

If you'd like to learn when I publish new books, please sign up for my Newsletter at www.eepurl.com/Rr31H. Again, I appreciate your interest and I hope you'll check out my other books.

Sincerely,
Geri Foster

CONTENTS

ACKNOWLEDGMENTS

This book is dedicated to my husband, Laurence Foster. After all these years you're still my one and only love. Thank you for your support, and for believing in me when I had doubts. You've shown me that dreams really do come true and love isn't just in romance novels.

Always,
Geri Foster

CHAPTER ONE

1947

Cora Williams-Carter had just finished baking an apple cobbler when Jack, her nephew, and her husband, Virgil Carter, came through the front door, dragging a huge Christmas tree behind them. Once inside, they closed the door, their faces beaming with pride.

"What do you think, Mom?" Jack asked, while Pal barked happily. Jack's mitten-covered hands clutched the bottom of the tree. "Didn't we get a good one?"

It still sounded strange for Jack to call her and Virgil Mom and Dad, but it also filled her with such love she simply couldn't explain how she felt. "My, it's really big."

"We can trim it down," Virgil offered. "It was the best one we found."

She moved to the living room, where they'd shoved furniture aside to make room for the tree to be displayed in front of the window. "Let's try to set it up here."

Kicking the tree stand in place, Virgil struggled to heave the tree upright, only for it to hit the ceiling and the top to bend over. "We're going to have to cut off more than I thought," he said, scratching his head.

"It sure didn't look this big when we were chopping it down," Jack said, his eyes tracing the massive height.

Pal barked and danced around the strange object that had been brought into his territory. Even he realized the tree wasn't going to work because it took up most of the living room.

"Let's get her outside and cut some off the bottom. Then we'll try again," Virgil said, as he worked to turn the tree around in the small space.

1

Cora jumped out of the way before one of the branches slapped her in the face. When she went to get the mop from the back porch, she ran into her neighbor Earl.

"What're you doing, Missy?"

"Virgil and Jack just came back with a Christmas tree and I'm going to mop up the melted snow."

Since removing his hat and coat, he relieved her of the mop. "Let me do that."

After learning she was pregnant, Earl thought she should be carried around on a pillow. Cora wondered how she could take five more months of that kind of treatment.

At the sound of the saw moving back and forth, she ran toward the front door. "Shake off all the snow before bringing it in next time."

Virgil pushed back his knit hat and smiled. "Sorry, we were so excited, we didn't think about that."

Glancing out, she noticed that only Jack's head rose above the limbs as he straddled the tree, holding it still for Virgil. A feeling of breathlessness washed over her. Christmas was such a magical time of the year for children and adults alike. This would be her first real Christmas, too.

Wiping her hands on her checkered apron, she smiled at the hard work the two were putting into making their home a cheerful place for the holidays.

Quite a contrast from the five years she'd spent behind the prison walls of the Women's Penitentiary of Missouri. There, one day melted into another, and joy and happiness were strangers to the miserable souls sentenced to a grueling existence.

At school, Jack had made garland from strips of construction paper glued together in rings, and several green Christmas trees with crayon-colored bulbs. Wanting to keep him busy inside since the weather had been absolutely miserable lately, she'd bought craft items for him to make angels from crepe paper to hang on the tree, and clothespins to paint like Santa and snowmen.

His art-work left a lot of room for improvement, but Jack was excited to have something he'd created on their first Christmas tree. The coming holidays had taken center stage in the conversations in their home since Thanksgiving Day. Now, with Santa and elves dancing in Jack's head, their home had become a busy and loud place to be.

The large box of ornaments from Earl's attic sat ready to be displayed on the tree. Earl and Virgil had struggled to get the container inside the house and in a place out of the way. Once they'd accomplished that, they went back for more. Even with a tree as big as Virgil had chopped down, there was more than enough to go on it.

After wiping up the floor, Earl propped the mop against the wall and helped Virgil and Jack bring the tree back in. It took several minutes to force it into the stand, but it still reached the ceiling. Some of the branches had lost so many needles already there were big gaps that had to be hidden against the wall.

Removing his hat, Virgil threw it on the couch and jammed his fists on his hip. "I never imagined it was that tall." He looked at Jack and winked. "Did you?"

Jack shook his head. "It looked pretty small next to the others."

The wonderful scent of cedar filled the small house and it certainly put Cora into a festive mood. "Let's have some hot chocolate and sugar cookies then we can tackle trimming that monster down to size."

As Virgil and Jack removed their coats and Earl cleaned the floor, she went into the kitchen and set a pan on the stove and a pot of coffee for her neighbor who wasn't fond of cocoa.

Putting out a plate of cookies, she hummed softly as the three in the living room argued about how to arrange things so they could walk to the door without hitting the tree. Stirring the cocoa slowly, Cora inhaled the delicious aroma of chocolate. Lately, she had been craving all sorts of sugary snacks.

With everyone around the table, she filled the cups with hot brews. Everyone had settled into their usual seats as Jack reached for a cookie.

Cocking a brow, Earl asked? "Did you wash your hands?"

"Yes, I did," Jack replied, proudly. "So don't go thinking you're getting a cookie before I do."

"Oh dear," Cora remarked. "Let's not start arguing about food, why don't we."

"No fuss," her neighbor commented. "Just keeping that youngster on the straight and narrow."

Virgil tried a sip of hot chocolate and graced her with a beautiful smile. "This is delicious."

"Everything she makes is top shelf," Earl snapped.

Virgil set down his cup. "Who put a burr under your saddle?" He reached for a cookie. "It's the holidays. Christmas is right around the corner."

"I just have a lot on my mind." Earl pinched his lips and stared out the kitchen window. "It's that time of year we have to figure out the town budget and ain't nothing adding up."

"What seems to be the problem?" Virgil asked, tilting his head to the side. "Anything I can help you with?"

"No." Earl shook his head. "I can figure it out." Earl was in charge of the town budget and at the end of the year, an informal audit was conducted. Her neighbor had been poring over numbers for the last two weeks.

"Good," Virgil said. "After what Gibbs City has been through, we don't need another problem."

"I agree," Cora said as she rose to get more drinks. "After the mine cave-in, Hilda being murdered, Ester kidnapped then Warren Hayes showing up, I could go for a little peace on earth."

"Yeah," Jack said around a mouthful of cookie. "No more trouble. I don't want to have to save Dad again."

Biting back a grin, Cora glanced sideways at her nephew and noticed his chest swell. He was pretty proud of himself for helping Virgil off Black Water Bridge safely. It had been quite a feat that required bravery and ingenuity, Jack had come through with admirable courage and made her proud and Virgil grateful. Cora gave thanks every day that they had both made it out alive.

Virgil reached over and clasped Jack's shoulder. "That's what a son's for. To always be there when you need him."

"Yelp," Jack agreed, nodding as he munched on another cookie.

"That's your last one, young man," Cora said. "You won't want dinner." She waved her hand at the huge tree that now leaned slightly toward the wall. "Plus, you and your dad have a big job to do."

They left her alone at the table while they approached the Christmas tree. Once again, it would have to be taken outside and cut back. She smiled at her happy family. Jack was off from school until after New Year's so she'd decided to stay home from work to be with him. It wasn't fair for Maggie to always be looking after him while she work when she missed being home so much.

She thought about the presents stashed at Earl's so Virgil and Jack wouldn't go prowling around looking for them. Jack had been easy to shop for; Virgil on the other hand had taken her forever.

A knock at the door had Earl opening it to find Patrick Maloney, the newly hired Hospital Administrator, standing on the front porch dressed in a finely tailored suit with his thick salt and pepper hair combed back neatly. Earl quickly shook hands with the man then introduced him to Virgil. "Cora recommended him as a replacement for Levy. The board was very impressed during his interview."

Patrick moved closer and Cora embraced him in a warm hug. He was in his early fifties, tall and lean with a head for managing hospitals. He'd done a great job in St. Louis and she felt he'd do as well for Gibbs City General.

Standing back, she smiled. "We're so glad you decided to come here. I'm sure you'll love it as much as Jack and I do."

His keen but soft brown eyes gave off a genuine feeling of trust. "I'm grateful for the opportunity. I promise the citizens of this town I'll make sure the hospital is run efficiently and offers the best care around."

"We can't ask for more." Cora stepped back and grinned at their new addition.

"Have you found a place to stay?" Virgil asked.

Patrick turned, gracing Virgil with a warm smile. "I've rented a small house on St. Francis Street. About two blocks away. It's furnished, so it'll do nicely."

Patrick had lost his wife to breast cancer when she was in her early forties, leaving him alone since her death. They hadn't had children and that made Cora wonder how lonely his life must be without family. Perhaps there in Gibbs City he could make friends and be content.

"Do you have plans for Christmas dinner?" she asked. "You're more than welcome here."

He shook his head. "I appreciate the offer, but I'll be with my brother's family in Mount Vernon. They always have a big to-do with eight children."

The emptiness in Patrick's eyes pulled at her heart and pain stretched across her chest. How sad to be alone this time of year.

Leaving Earl and Jack to trim the tree, Virgil joined them in the kitchen. Leaning against the sink, he said, "The hospital really needs someone who can put us back on track and get along with the employees. Our last guy was a tyrant."

"I'd met him before and knew immediately he had no business bring an administrator." Patrick smiled at Virgil. "Gibbs City General will find me much easier to work with. I promise."

Waving her hand toward the table, Cora offered, "Coffee and cookies?"

"No, I just wanted to stop by and say thank you for recommending me for the job. I really appreciate your trust in me."

She patted him on the arm. "You'll do fine. And we need someone like you who is approachable and can be reasoned with."

She watched him shake hands with Earl again before leaving.

"He seems like a nice guy," Virgil said.

She stared at the front door. "From my experience, he's very good at his job and he's a problem solver."

"Unlike Levy," Earl said.

Rolling her eyes, she said, "Oh, let's not talk about him. I was glad to see him go."

"We all were," Virgil said. She followed her husband's gaze to the Christmas tree. "I sure wish we'd cut down a smaller tree."

"Looks like your eyes were bigger than our living room."

He laughed. "Something like that."

A knock sounded at the back door. Before anyone could answer, Jack's friend, Tommy Cox, plowed his way through the kitchen. Pal barked at his heels all the way to the living room.

Tommy came to a halt in front of the tree. "Wow." Tommy's eyes widened. "That's a big tree."

"I know," Jack said, proudly. "Me and Dad dragged it all the way back to where we were parked. It took us a long time to tie it to the roof of the car."

"That's going to look good when you get it decorated."

"Well," Jack said, "we can't even start until we get the darn thing to fit in here right."

Tommy cocked his head. "What's wrong with it?"

"Mom says it's too big."

Tommy shook his head. "No, it's not."

"That's what I say," Jack agreed. "But you know moms."

"Yeah, my mom made us get a small one. She wouldn't even let us in the door with the big one my brothers had chopped down. And she's already complaining about sweeping up the needles."

Earl knelt down so he'd be eyelevel with the children. "You boys all ready for the school play?"

Tommy's face turned sour. "We ain't going."

Surprised, Earl sat back on his heels. "Why not?"

Jack brushed needles off his shirt. "Cause we ain't in nothing. We just got to paint the rocks behind the people on stage."

"Neither of you got a part in the play?"

"No," Tommy said. His bottom lip stuck out. "We don't even get to be on stage."

"What about being a shepherd?" Earl scowled.

"Not a blasted thing," Jack said loudly. "We're just going to be standing with the class when they sing three songs."

"Yeah," Tommy said. "That ain't even worth going for."

"Well, I'll be," Earl said, looking off into the distance. "Used to be every kid had some part."

"Not anymore," Jack said.

A kid being left out of the school's Christmas play didn't set will with Earl Clevenger. He wasted little time putting on his winter coat and leaving Cora and Virgil's house in search of Miss Potter, the school teacher.

At her small home on Liberty Street, he pounded on the door. She answered with a bright smile. "Hello, Mr. Clevenger. It's nice to see you. Won't you come in?"

"I ain't got time. I came here to find out why Jack and Tommy aren't in the Christmas play?"

Her lips tightened and her chin came up. "I simply didn't have a part for them. Besides, I'm sure you're concerned because you like those two boys, but they have to learn they can't be in everything."

Stomping the snow off his boots, Earl announced, "There was a time when every kid was in that pageant. Those who didn't have real parts were angels and shepherds."

She shook her head in determination. "We didn't do that this year. I thought the stage would be too crowded."

Earl narrowed his eyes at the skinny, plain-looking young woman who needed to get rid of that prideful look on her face. "I don't like it."

She folded her arms in front of her and tried to smile, but she looked like a chicken ready to be plucked. "I understand you're on the school board, but these things are left to me and I've made my decision." She tried to sound cheerful, but failed. "Besides, the play is only a couple of days away. This is no time for changes."

He pointed a finger at her. "There are plenty of shepherd and angel costumes from you throwing a fit two years ago because you thought it only fair that every kid got to be in the play. We spent a fortune at your request."

"That was then." She raised her nose and voice. "I have the right to change things if I want to."

"You get all those kids in school on that stage for the play or you'll be looking for a job next year."

She stepped back, clutching her sweater. "You can't come to my house threatening me like that."

He turned to leave. "I ain't threatening. But I better see the whole school on that stage or you're out of here."

Damn stupid woman. Kids lived for that kind of stuff. He bet she only chose her favorites to be up there for everyone to see. Well, he wouldn't stand for it. Not from her, anyway.

On his way back home, Earl saw Arthur coming out of the dry cleaners. He waved. "What are you doing out and about?" Earl asked, shivering. "I figured you'd be home sipping a nice glass of brandy."

Arthur laughed. "You're just the man I'm looking for." His friend nudged him lightly on the shoulder. "Are you in the mood to go shopping for toys?"

Earl forgot all about Miss Potter as his heart grew lighter. "Is that today?"

Arthur winked at him and grinned mysteriously. "We have to get everything so the ladies of the Prayer Committee will have time to wrap the presents so we can get them under the tree."

Earl looked at the town square and the tall tree they'd decorated for the holiday. Soon they'd all gather around as he and Arthur passed out presents that Santa had left for the children of Gibbs City. "You got the list?"

His friend pulled a folded sheet of paper out of his pocket and waved it in the air. "We'll be busy."

"You check with JJ?"

"He dropped off the names of the colored children needing presents yesterday."

Earl hooked his arm in Arthur's elbow and waltzed toward his friend's fancy automobile. "We'd better get going." He opened the car door. "We might need a trailer to get everything back to town."

Arthur looked around. "I hope it's dark when we unload all those toys. It would be sad if a child saw *Santa* bringing toys into my house."

"We've been doing this for years and never been caught. Earl rubbed his hands together. "This is my favorite time of year."

CHAPTER TWO

Virgil watched as Jack and his friend Tommy decorated the Christmas tree as far up as they could reach. Tommy's mother, Maggie, sat in the kitchen enjoying coffee with Cora. A knock sounded at the door. He opened it to find little Ronnie Hayes with his adoptive mother, Susan.

"Come in, what are you two doing out today?"

Susan smiled. "Ronnie made a special ornament for your tree and wanted to bring it over."

"Hi, Susan," Cora called out. "Come join us in the kitchen."

Ronnie greeted his friends and they went about hooking bulbs on the tree. Kneeling next to Pal, Virgil and the dog watched the boys laughing and teasing each other. They'd formed a special bond since Jack and Cora had arrived in Gibbs City. Every young boy needed to create friendships. Some would last a lifetime, like his and Carl's. Buford, too. They'd been friends since the first grade.

He'd no sooner started untangling the lights when another knock landed on the door. Exchanging surprised glances with Cora, he stood and opened the door. The school teacher, Miss Ruth Potter, stood on his porch, a bag of clothes in her hand.

"Hello, Ruth, won't you come in?"

"No, I came to drop these off." She held out the bag. "Tell Jack he's in the school play."

"I don't want to be in anything," Jack said as he continued to decorate the tree. "I don't want to be in no dumb play."

Cora, Maggie and Susan walked into the living room. "Hello, Ruth," Cora said. "What's this about the play?"

"I'm glad you're all here. That will save me time. Here are your kid's

9

costumes for the play so they can be in it. They'll be elves and can stand in the back with the others."

"What?" Maggie asked. "Our boys are the only ones who were not in the play?"

Ruth Potter blinked hard, took a deep breath then lifted her chin. "Yes, I was afraid the stage would be so crowded that one of the children might fall off. But Mr. Clevenger came over earlier and informed me that all the students would participate."

Virgil put his hands on his hips and frowned. "You're the one two years ago who told the council you wanted every child to be in the play."

"I did. But this year I changed my mind."

Susan stepped forward. "Why?"

Ruth turned aside. "I hold no grudge against your boys, it just turned out that they were the ones not in the play."

The three boys came closer and lined up in front of their teacher. Tommy spoke. "We don't want to be in the play and we're not dressing up like elves "cause we ain't gonna be there."

Jack backed him up. "You should've let Ronnie be the baby Jesus because he's the smallest, but you chose a girl. That's when we decided we weren't going to be in no play."

Cora held up her hands. "Jack, please, I won't allow you to be rude." She looked at the school teacher. "What's going on here?"

Tommy scrunched up his face and pointed at Miss Potter. "She don't like Ronnie."

"That isn't true. Not at all," the school teacher stuttered, trying to defend herself against the accusation.

Susan pulled Ronnie back against her. "You don't like my son? You're treating him differently? How dare you."

"That's not true," Ruth insisted.

Virgil knelt down in front of the boys. "Why do you think she doesn't like Ronnie?"

"She called him a spoiled brat for no reason at all," Jack said, putting his arm around his friend. "Ronnie isn't a brat."

"I didn't say it like that." Her lips puckered in a stubborn frown. "I said, 'don't act like a spoiled brat'. Ronnie was misbehaving and disrupting the class."

Jack looked Virgil in the eye, his expression serious. "Yes, she don't like none of us. And sometimes she don't let him go out for recess for doing nothing."

"You misunderstood. I'm not picking on the child," Ruth Potter declared.

Susan's cheeks flushed pink. "I want to know exactly why you've singled out my child, Miss Potter. And you better have a good reason."

"I'm not."

Virgil stepped between the two women. "If there's a problem here, it's best if we let the school board decide." He opened the door. "Miss Potter, I'll notify Paul Russell there's to be a meeting sometime during the holiday break. In the meantime, my son won't be participating."

"Neither will ours," Maggie and Susan echoed.

Hands balled, Ruth Potter exited the house with her face stormy and her posture stiff.

Afterwards, Jack was happy to go out and play with Tommy and Ronnie. Decorating a tree was fun, but being outside in the snow was a lot more fun.

Pal liked lying in front of the stove and staying warm today, so Jack left him behind. He thought maybe Pal was tired from running around the forest while they looked for a Christmas tree.

Jack knew his neighborhood well. He was familiar with every person's house. And since he often had Pal with him, they made a bunch of friends. While his pooch liked other dogs, he didn't like when they got too close.

Mr. Hickmen always waved when he was outside and sometimes had them wait for a couple of Mrs. Hickman's cookies. Old man Gizer was ancient, but not nice like his Uncle Earl. He was grouchy and would shake his his cane at them just for walking down the sidewalk. But that didn't scare Jack since the old man never stepped off his porch.

As the boys made their way to Grover's Grocery Store they laughed, rolled in the snow and had a snowball fight. But none of them were very good at hitting much of anything and that included each other. At the store, they went inside to spend the money his dad had given him.

Each sucking on a candy cane, Jack grinned, remembering how his dad had whispered man to man that if he bought sweets, he still had to eat all his supper tonight. That wouldn't be hard because Jack always felt hungry and his mom was the best cook in the world.

Before leaving the house, they had been instructed not to go any farther than the grocery store, or do anything else. That included staying out of the slippery streets. His dad had told him not to be long.

But in Jack's mind, that didn't mean they couldn't play along the way. Ronnie liked to play cowboys and Indians while Tommy liked cops and robbers. Jack loved Superman best. He helped people and always made things okeydokey in the end.

Looking up, Jack noticed it was snowing again. He was glad, since Christmas was so close. He'd written his letter to Santa but he hadn't asked for much. Mostly he wanted them to be a family forever and a new bike would be great as well.

Enjoying their treats, Ronnie, Tommy and Jack were making their way down Pearl Street when a car pulled up and stopped. A man rolled down the window and told Jack to get inside. His mom and dad had told him not to talk to strangers or get into a car with someone he didn't know. Fear climbed down his back and his muscles tightened.

"I can't," Jack said. "My folks won't like it."

"Do what you're told," the man shouted. "Don't make me have to get out of this car with it snowing."

Stepping up the pace, Jack looked back. "I ain't going nowhere with you, mister. My dad's the Sheriff. You better leave me alone."

"You get back here."

Tommy put his hand on the back of Jack's coat and grabbed Ronnie by the hand. "Let's run."

The three dashed to the corner, cut through the Reynolds' yard, darted between Mrs. Hitchcock's house and the Martin's then rounded the Jasper's fence. With a quick glance behind them, they sped to the back of Shuster's shed. They squatted down, breathing hard as they hugged each other and listened for the sound of footsteps.

After several minutes, Ronnie went to stand, but Jack heard something, grabbed him by the coat and pulled him back down. With his finger to his lips, they crouched low.

Complete silence filled the air and Jack wished he'd brought Pal with him. Ronnie began to tremble but he kept his hand over his mouth to keep quiet and not give away their position.

Ronnie's boot slid against the fence, making it shake. They waited, heads bowed.

Suddenly Jack was grabbed by the back of his coat and swung up. He screamed as loud as he could and kicked his feet furiously. "Let me go," he screamed. "Let me go."

Tommy punched the man in the leg and stomped on his foot, but the stranger knocked him away. Ronnie caught up with the bad man and made a dive toward his leg. Biting down hard as he could, he hung on with all his might.

The man screamed and kicked Ronnie away, but Tommy was already pelting the bad guy with snowballs and anything else he could get his hands on. With Jack squirming and kicking, a snowball hit his attacker in the head, and little Ronnie kept trying to trip the man.

Finally, he stumbled against Mrs. Reynolds' porch, gasping for air. "You're a lot of trouble, kid."

"Let me go. My dad's gonna be really mad."

The man shook Jack furiously. "Your daddy don't scare me. Now shut up before I tie a gag over your mouth."

Taking huge steps, the man headed back to the car with a mean look on his face. Jack was scared and he wished he were home where it was safe. Suddenly, a big snowball slapped the burly guy right in the face, nearly knocking him to the ground.

Jack quickly unbuttoned his coat and slid out of the garment. The three boys took off in the direction of Jack's house with the stranger catching up fast and shouting for them to stop.

Then as Jack looked back, he saw the giant of a man slide on the slippery sidewalk and fall on his backside. Clutching Ronnie's hand, they ran as fast as they could. But Jack knew it wouldn't be long before the man caught them. They'd never make it to his house.

Seeing Granny Riley sweeping snow off her porch, the boys ran up her stairs. "Help! A man's after us."

She looked around then shoved them inside. Backs against the wall near the door, Jack gasped for air as his friends shook and trembled with fear.

Granny Riley was the mother of his dad's friend, Carl, and he liked her a lot. She was scrawny like a wet chicken, but she was not someone people in town messed with. He'd once heard his mom and Aunt Maggie talking about the time she threw a brick through Grover's Grocery Store because her paper sack tore open on the way home.

"I ain't seen nothing," Jack heard Granny Riley say. "Whatcha doing out here, running around in the snow like a fool?"

The man who'd tried to grab him was standing right outside on the sidewalk. Jack peeked through the crack in the door at the stranger. A mean frown marred his ugly face.

"There were three of them. You had to have seen them run by."

Granny Riley picked up her broom and held it like a bat. "You calling me a liar?"

"No, but I don't know how you missed them." He swung his hand. "They came this way."

"Well," Granny Riley said. "If you're looking for three boys, why don't you check at Sheriff Carter's office?" She swept a bunch of snow toward the man. "You ain't even from around here, are you? I've never seen you afore."

"That's none of your business."

Mr. Garrett, across the street, opened his door and walked to the edge of his porch. "What's going on, Granny Riley?"

"This man thinks I'm a liar."

"I didn't say that," the foreigner hollered

"Say's he's chasing three boys."

"Why, he ain't got no business chasing nobody in this town." Mr. Garrett returned to his house and came out with a rifle. "Whatcha wanting with those kids anyway? You best be on your way, stranger."

Relief weakened Jack's legs and he feared he might crumble to the floor. Mr. Garrett came across the street and watched the man walk back toward his car parked on Pearl Street.

When the guy who'd been after them was out of sight, Granny Riley said to Mr. Garrett. "You go home and call Sheriff Carter. One of the boys he was chasing was his boy. The Cox's kid and that little Ronnie the Welches adopted are with him." She moved along the porch looking between the houses. "Tell the sheriff to get here fast. That man ain't leaving."

Granny Riley came in the house and locked the door. "You boys follow me." She walked toward the kitchen. Once there, she lifted a rug to reveal a trap-door in the floor. "Get down there and don't come out until your daddy comes to get you. Don't be scared. It's just a root cellar. Ain't nothing down there to hurt you."

Sophia Riley never went looking for trouble but she never ran from it either. She considered herself kind, and believed in justice and fair play. Any man trying to kidnap children didn't deserve her kindness. No, he warranted her old scatter gun.

Going into the bedroom she'd shared with her dearly departed husband for over fifty years, she pulled out his old World War I rifle. It showed its age, but her son Carl, out of respect for his father, had maintained the gun and she knew it worked. She'd killed plenty of rabbits who visited her garden in the summer. Those varmints ended up in her cooking pot and had made for fine suppers.

Knowing the gun was loaded, she went to her front window and looked out the edge of the curtain. A car she'd never seen stood parked outside her house, as if the man was trying to decide if he wanted to come in or not. He wasn't going away and the sheriff wasn't there yet.

Unlocking the door quietly, Sophia stuck the barrel of her weapon out the crack and fired. Her neighbor fired his gun and blew out the tires. She fired again and hit the side of the door. Inside the car, the man ducked down in the seat to keep from getting his brains blown out.

In the distance, the sound of sirens filled the air and loosened Sophia's muscles. Satisfied she'd kept the culprit from escaping, she watched as Virgil came from one end of the street and Deputy Ethan from the other.

When they stopped, she put the gun down and ran to let the boys out of the cellar. They were shaking in their boots, for sure. Probably from being chased and then stuffed in a dark cellar. But she had no choice. That man was up to no good, and if she'd wanted to keep them alive, she'd had to keep them out of sight.

Virgil got out of his car with his gun drawn.

Sophia gathered the boys close. "Stay inside. Don't come out until it's safe."

She stepped on the porch with her gun pointed at the parked car. "He came running up to my house saying he was looking for three boys, Sheriff."

"Where are the boys?"

"In my house, safe and sound."

"Keep them there." She watched as Virgil went to the driver side of the car and told the stranger to get out. When he refused, Virgil used the butt of his gun to knock out the window, unlock the door and drag the man out by his collar.

Ethan had a gun on the man, and Sophia knew he'd shoot at a moment's provocation. That stranger who'd come to their town with meanness on his mind would be real smart to own up to whatever nonsense he'd been up to rather than have Virgil take him to the jailhouse. One thing about the sheriff, you best not mess with him.

He was tough, righteous and mean as a pissed-off rattler when he was mad. Right now, he was mad enough to beat that man twice his size half to death without breaking a sweat.

"Start explaining yourself. What do you want with these boys?"

"I ain't saying a word except I want a lawyer."

"That's fine. We're going to take you to the station so you can use the phone, but I promise I'll get the truth out of you." Virgil shoved the guy to the ground and slapped the handcuffs on him. "Get in the squad car or I'll tie you to the bumper and drag you. Believe me, I'd prefer the latter."

The man grumbled, but he did as he was told. "Mr. Garrett, you keep your gun on him. He acts like he wants to get out of my cruiser, blow his head off."

Jim moved closer. Sophia suspected as ornery as her neighbor was, he probably hoped the prisoner would do something foolish just so he could shoot him. As Virgil and Ethan came toward her house, she pushed open the door, and the three boys ran into his arms.

Now that is was over, they were boo-hooing all over the place. Virgil just held them tight against his chest until they settled down.

Wiping their faces and noses, the three stood in front of him trying to explain everything at once. "I was scared, Dad. More scared than I'd ever been," Jack said.

"Where's your coat, Son?"

"That man grabbed me up by the back of my jacket. I undid the buttons so I could slide out of it and ran. It's in Mrs. Reynolds' yard."

"You boys go with Ethan. Get your coat, Jack, then he's going to take you home."

Ronnie pointed to his squad car. "Is he gonna come after us again?" the young boy asked. "I can't run that fast, Uncle Virgil." Ronnie ducked his head. "Um, Uncle Virgil, I bit that man. Am I in trouble?"

"No." Virgil put his hand on the boy's shoulder. "You were a very brave boy, Ronnie. You all were. And none of you will ever see that man again."

They filed out huddling close to Ethan. Virgil glanced back at Sophia, fighting the tears gathering in his eyes. He pulled her into his arms and hugged her tightly, his body trembling, a sick feeling gathering in the pit of his gut. "Thank you so much, Mrs. Riley. No other person would've done what you did today."

She stepped away, fighting against her own tears. "Aw, you know better than that. Ain't a citizen in Gibbs City who'd let anyone come in this town and hurt a child."

"I know, but thank you anyway. Your quick thinking made all the difference."

She smiled and patted him on the cheek like she had when he was a little boy. "My pleasure."

CHAPTER THREE

Cora hugged her arms to keep her hands from shaking as she waited on the porch with Maggie and Susan. Virgil had only told them to wait where they were. He also mentioned that someone had been chasing the boys.

"They'll be okay," Maggie said. "That boy of mine is fast as lightning."

Susan sniffed. "Mine's not. Little Ronnie can't keep up with Tommy and Jack."

Cora put her arm around Susan. "They'd never run off and leave him behind. They're like brothers."

They turned at the sound of an approaching car. When she saw Ethan driving toward them with the boys in the backseat of the vehicle, Cora nearly wept with joy. By the time he stopped in front of the house, the women were at the curb greeting their children.

"You're cold as ice," Susan said when she lifted Ronnie into her arms. "Let's get you inside."

"Are you okay, Jack?" Cora asked. "Did anyone hurt you?"

"No, Granny Riley hid us in her cellar and got out her gun."

"Oh, Lord," Maggie said. "Did she kill anyone?"

"No, but she shot a few times," Tommy added. "She's a tough old bird."

"Tommy Cox," Maggie scolded, taking her son by the shoulder. "You stop repeating your father's words."

"It's true," Ronnie said. "She saved us."

Inside, coats and boots came off and the boys sat at the table with warm apple cider and cookies.

Earl came through the door, without wearing a jacket, hat or his boots. "What's this about a kidnapper in town?"

Ethan leaned against the sink. "Earl, I was just headed to your house. You get Arthur, Leonard, Briggs, and anyone else you can think of and comb the town. I'm getting Carl, Buford, JJ and Ben. Virgil wants to know if this guy's working alone or if he brought help."

Earl strode purposely to the phone in the living room. "You get a move on and I'll put a gang together." He pressed the receiver to his chest. "What happened?"

"Some man tried to kidnap Jack," Ethan said.

The look on Earl's face would scare the devil. "What?"

"Virgil's taking him to the station. We want to make sure there's only one."

Earl put the phone to his ear. "Arthur, get over here and pick me up. We're going looking for someone who tried to kidnap one of our kids." He paused. "Yes, bring every gun you have. Somebody needs killing."

He hugged the young boys then turned to Susan. "You stay here until I get Briggs to see you home safely." Then he stomped out the door, his jaw tight.

Cora held Jack, afraid to let him go. The thought that someone would steal him away sent her mind reeling and had chills running up and down her back. Squeezing him gently, she didn't know what she'd do without Jack.

As the boys enjoyed their warm drinks and rehashed their near abduction, Maggie, Susan and Cora sat in stunned silence as they tried to rationalize what'd happened.

Cora squeezed Susan's hand. "Maybe you should keep little Ronnie away from Jack until this is straightened out."

"No," Ronnie shouted. "He's my friend and he saved me today. I'm not staying away."

Susan smoothed down the hair on her son's head. "We'll see how all this goes. I wouldn't think about keeping you away from your friends during this time of year, but we have to be careful." She looked into his warm brown eyes. "Until we know what's going on, we want you safe. You understand, don't you?"

Ronnie nodded, but the sadness pulling at his face showed his concern for not being able to visit his friends.

Maggie stood. "Tommy and I are going to run home while Briggs is still there." She patted Susan on the shoulder. "It will all be fine."

Ronnie and Jack raced into the living room and hopped on the couch with a warm blanket covering them. The radio was on, but Cora didn't think they were listening. Instead, she imagined they replayed the events of the day over and over in their minds.

She wanted to talk to Virgil and find out who was behind this. Who would come here and try to kidnap Jack? Certain names came to mind, but it would be so reckless of them to do something like trying to take their son away from them.

Soon Briggs arrived and walked Susan and an exhausted Ronnie home. He instructed Cora to stay inside with the doors locked. Everyone would use precautions, but she knew it was Jack who had been the target and she had a good idea who was behind it all.

She peeked into the living room as she cleared the table. She straightened, considering the tree, with its sparkling lights and haphazard decorations. What kind of Christmas would they have this year? Gripping the edge of the table, she realized if Dan and Ann kept trying to take Jack away, her family would be on pins and needles until it all ended.

Alone, Jack huddled in the corner of the couch, Pal on his lap, licking his face, apparently trying to bring him comfort. As shock set in, his normally bright face was solemn and pale. The typically busy little boy sat motionless, wrapped in fear. No child should live like that.

She lowered herself on the couch and pulled him against her. His little body trembled, making her want to strike back at those who'd tried to harm him. She snuggled beneath the blanket with him and he rested his head on her chest.

"You okay, Jack?"

"I'm fine, Mom."

"You're brave, but I know you can't have a man chasing you and then be fine."

"Well," he looked up at her and wrinkled his nose, "I might have been a little scared. But I knew Dad would come and take care of that bad guy. He won't be hurting nobody else."

"You're right." She leaned down and kissed him on the nose. "Everything's going to be just fine. You can count on your dad to make certain you're safe. I'm proud of you. You and your friends did the right thing. Just like Superman."

Cora had no doubt Virgil would settle the matter about the man who'd tried to kidnap Jack, and that monster would never frighten an innocent child again.

CHAPTER FOUR

Virgil arrived at the station and unloaded the man who'd tried to take his son away, and he was none too gentle about it, either. After searching the pockets of his prisoner and finding a crumpled piece of paper with their address on it, a picture of a younger Jack, and a loaded pistol in his coat, Virgil took out his driver's license and threw the contents onto the table.

Shoving the shackled man into a nearby chair, Virgil moved to Ethan's desk and took out a pad and pencil. He picked up the license. "Okay, Harley Marshall Bremen, what brings you to Gibbs City?"

"I want to call my lawyer." He rolled his upper lip into a snarl. "I'm not saying a word."

Virgil reached into his pocket and removed the keys and unlocked the cuffs. While Bremen rubbed his wrists, Virgil looked at the contents on the desk. He bit back a growl of anger. To think that this man brought a gun to kidnap his son made Virgil so angry he no longer trusted himself.

"Do you admit that this is your correct name?"

"Go to hell," the man spat. "You think some little Podunk town like this is going to do anything to me? I'll have this place torn apart before Christmas Day."

"About that call," Virgil said, picking up the phone. "Here it is." Instead of handing the phone to the prisoner, Virgil shoved the whole thing into his face so hard, his chair tipped over.

With the bruiser on the floor, Virgil kicked the man in the shoulder and stomach then stomped on his face. He grabbed him by the front of his coat, pulled him up and slammed his fist into the center of the man's face. Bones crunched.

The stranger swung wildly, but Virgil ducked and with his entire body weight behind him, he slammed his fist into the man's gut and up into his stomach. Harley Marshall Bremen buckled over and fell forward.

Virgil caught him and gave him a right jab and a left hook. Bleeding from his mouth and nose, Harley staggered against the wall and held up his hands. Knowing that scum had chased after three frightened little boys, Virgil grabbed him by the hair and slammed his head back.

Bremen fell, sprawled out unconscious on the floor. For good measure, Virgil gave him one last kick to the side of the head.

He'd just washed his hands and splashed water on his face when Ethan walked in with Earl. "What happened here?" Earl asked, looking down at the out-cold man.

"He stumbled getting out of the car." Virgil tossed the towel aside. "You find anyone else?"

"Not a soul," Earl said, passing the driver's license to Ethan.

Virgil waved his bruised hand at the deputy. "Help me get him sitting upright."

They dragged the heavy man to the wooden, ladder-backed chair. After plopping him down, Virgil filled up the empty coffee pot with water and threw it on the man's battered face. Anger still boiled inside him.

"Ethan," Virgil said, "Mr. Garret drove Bremen's car to the station. I want you to search it and see what you can find. See if anything can explain why he's in our town."

The man sputtered and swung his arms wildly but he was too weak to stand. "What happened?"

"We were just talking about how you were going to tear my little Podunk town apart before Christmas."

"I want to call my lawyer."

"You're in need of more than a lawyer. I think your jaw is broken. Your nose is for sure," Virgil stated.

"You can't treat a man like this."

Virgil walked over, leaned close and hissed, "You come into my county to kidnap my son, and you sit there telling me what I can and can't do?"

"It's the law."

"Oh, now you want to talk about the law." He turned away. "You lost every privilege you're entitled to when you scared the hell out of three little boys." Virgil tapped his chest. "And you were after mine."

"I want my phone call."

Earl walked over and kicked the chair out from under him, and slammed his foot down on the man's throat. "Who sent you?"

"I'm not saying nothing."

Earl took his pocket knife out of his pocket, flipped the blade open and flicked his thumb over the edge. "Still nice and sharp." He held up the weapon. "Let's start by cutting off a few fingers."

"No," the man screamed, jamming his fist between his legs. "You people can't do this."

Virgil looked down at the bleeding man and shrugged. "My town, my rules."

"You have to give me a phone call," Bremen screamed. He acted as if fear had crawled inside him and was eating him alive.

"Not after what you've done." Virgil glanced at Earl's knife. "I'm all for letting you carve him up and after he bleeds to death, we'll take him to McGregor's old mine-shaft and throw his body in there."

"Yeah," Earl chuckled, waving the knife in front of Bremen's face. "Nobody will ever find a trace."

Virgil grabbed the chair, dragged the man into the seat and spun him around. "Why are you here?"

"Go to hell."

Ethan came through the door holding up a bag. "I found this in the glove compartment. Looks like about fifteen hundred dollars."

Virgil kicked back the chair, slamming Bremen's head on the hard floor. "Who are you working for, you bastard? Who sent you?"

"I'm not talking."

"Oh, you'll talk all right. You're going to sing like a bird." He looked at Ethan. "Go get Judge Garner." He looked down at Bremen spread-eagle on the floor. "Take your time."

Earl stomped on Bremen's hand, crushing it beneath his heel. The man screamed so loud, Virgil wondered how long it'd be before he lost his voice.

Bending down, Earl nicked the corner of Bremen's nose with his knife. "We have all the time in the world."

"You people are crazy." Desperate for the punishment to stop, the man raised a bloody hand in surrender, "Please stop and I'll tell you everything. I promise."

Taking him by each arm, Earl and Virgil helped the man back in the chair. Virgil went behind the desk and picked up a pencil. "Start by giving me the name of the person who sent you here."

"It was Ann Martin and her son, Dan."

Virgil and Earl shared an angry glare. "How much did they pay you?"

"They gave me fifteen hundred dollars up front to get the boy, and promised another two thousand when I deliver him."

Virgil spun the tablet around and handed the prisoner the pencil. "Sign it."

"I can't." He nodded toward Earl. "He broke my hand."

"Use the other."

After signing the confession, the man asked to make a phone call again, but Virgil didn't want to let him breathe, much less give him his rights.

The judge entered behind Ethan, and came to a halt. "I heard there was a stranger in town."

"Armed with a gun, this man came to Gibbs City and chased Jack, Ronnie and Tommy to Mrs. Riley's house. She managed to hold him off." He glanced back at the bruised and battered man. Virgil picked up the notebook. "He signed a confession saying that Ann and Dan Martin hired him to do the job."

The judge remained quiet for a few minutes then he took off his hat and coat and picked up the receiver. "Get him some medical attention and then lock him up." Garner looked at Bremen. "You're under arrest for attempted kidnapping, disturbing the peace, and jeopardizing the lives of three children."

"I wasn't going to hurt them."

"Then why are you carrying a gun? For all we know you were paid to murder Jack Martin," Earl shouted.

"I wouldn't kill a kid."

Judge Garner lifted a brow. "But you'd gladly steal him away from his family at Christmas time, not knowing what hell you'd be sending that child into?"

Bremen shook his head and blinked several times. "I didn't think they'd hurt the boy."

Earl walked over. "But you didn't know for sure, did you? After what happened to that poor Lindbergh baby, kidnapping's now a federal offense. You have to be plumb stupid to agree to do this."

While the judge talked on the phone, Virgil went to his cruiser and called for the attending medical assistant to come to the jail and check out the prisoner.

When he came back inside, Earl and the judge had their heads together. Looking up, Judge Garner said, "I have an arrest warrant for Ann and her son waiting in St. Louis. You go there and see that they're taken into custody."

"I'll contact Batcher right away." Virgil thumbed behind his shoulder. "What about him?"

"He stays here until he looks better," Judge Garner answered.

"Said he wants a phone call."

Judge Garner reached down and pulled the phone wire out of the wall. "It's not working. We can still receive calls on the radio in your cruiser." The judge nodded toward the phone. "When we get that fixed the day after Christmas, we'll let him make his call then."

Earl looked at Bremen and smiled. "Looks like he's going to miss Santa."

Ethan frowned. "He's going to miss a hell of a lot more than that."

CHAPTER FIVE

Cora and Jack were still on the couch when Virgil came in. "What happened," she asked, coming to her feet. "Is Jack safe?"

He reached down and hugged their tired son tightly to his chest. "He's fine."

Cora leaned down. "Jack, sweetheart, why don't you and Pal take a nap here on the sofa." He was so worn out from the excitement that he was already half asleep. Kissing his forehead, she pulled the blanket over him, the dog plastered to his side.

Feeling there were things that Virgil wanted to say but not in front of Jack, she said, "Come in the kitchen. I'll heat up some coffee."

Out of ear-shot, Virgil pulled Cora into his arms and held on to her desperately. "The Martins sent a man with a gun to kidnap Jack."

Cora's heart froze momentarily as she struggled to breathe. How on earth could they do such a thing to a little boy? Brushing away tears of fear, she said, "I was afraid that's what this was all about."

"I have an arrest warrant for them waiting in St. Louis. I plan to take those two monsters into custody. I'm leaving so I can be there before it gets late."

Glancing out at the early afternoon sun hidden behind gray skies, Cora moved quickly to pull things out of the icebox. "I'll fix you some sandwiches and hot coffee." As she busied herself, Virgil went into the bedroom. Cora hated that he'd be away so close to Christmas. What if he was detained?

She couldn't stand the thought of her and Jack spending Christmas without Virgil. Tears filled her eyes. By the time she had a sack lunch fixed with sandwiches, cheese and crackers, and several cookies, he'd come back into the room. She filled his thermos with hot coffee then tightened the cap.

She looked down at his empty hands and noticed his cracked knuckles. "What happened?"

"Nothing, just a little persuasion, that's all. I had to know why that guy wanted to kidnap Jack."

She kissed his hands. "It's amazing the things you do for your family." She looked down. "Where is your overnight bag?"

"I'll probably drive back late tonight."

"No, you won't," she said gruffly. "This could take longer than you plan and I don't want you driving in the dead of night, beat tired. You could have an accident."

"I hate to leave you and Jack overnight."

"Nonsense," Earl said, walking through the back door. "I'll watch over them. "Sides, the weather's miserable out there. You don't need to be sliding off the road and ending up in a ditch somewhere." Picking up the coffee pot, he looked for a cup. "Me and Arthur went to Joplin earlier." He winked. "We did our Santa run."

Looking outside, Cora realized Earl was right about Virgil being on the roads late at night. The snow hadn't let up much since earlier when the boys went to the grocery store for candy. "Listen to Earl. Jack and I will be fine. And I'll sleep better knowing you're not out there driving in a blizzard to get to us."

"Okay, I'll grab a bag and I'll call you when I get to a hotel."

She smiled through her misery. "That makes me feel so much better." She winked at Earl.

As she saw Virgil off with a promise that he'd be careful, and a scorching goodbye kiss, she and Earl sat at the kitchen table sipping coffee. "I can't believe those two would resort to something so sinister."

Earl shook his head. "And I wouldn't trust anyone alone with that Bremen guy. He's mean. God only knows what could've happened to those boys. Ronnie's going to have a black eye. That little tiger tried to bite a hunk out of Bremen's leg. Got thrown off and hit his face. Why, he could've been killed. Those boys fought mighty hard."

Cora rubbed her face. "I know. Maggie and Susan are worried sick."

"Well, Virgil will see those two in St. Louis spend Christmas in jail where they need to be.

"I hope it's that simple. I want him back home where he belongs. I don't trust Ann or Dan."

"Your husband is a man who can take care of himself." Earl rose. "I think I'm going home for a nap. What's for dinner?"

"Leftover pot roast and chocolate cake."

Earl's face lit up and his eyes darted toward the cupboards. "You got a cake hidden around here?"

She lightly slapped his hand. "Not until dinner."

Stretching tiredly, she thought briefly of the laundry she had to do, but Jack was waking up from his nap and she felt more like spending time with him on the floor playing cards. He'd gotten a deck of Old Maid and had become pretty good at the game.

She popped some popcorn, and poured them some cider as they sat on the living room rug with Pal between them. The snow had let up some, but the windows were frosted over and the smell of cinnamon and cedar filled the little house.

They'd been playing for about half an hour when a knock sounded at the door. Jack stiffened and wrapped his arms around a growling Pal. Carefully Cora walked to the door and looked out. JJ stood on the porch.

She opened up, glad to see him. After pulling him into a tight hug, she said, "What brings you out in this weather?"

He handed her a folder and removed his coat. "Let's talk in the kitchen."

The place she prepared meals was becoming a confessional. She waved the papers on the way to the back of the house. "What's this?"

"The last thing I ever expected."

She stopped dead in her tracks and turned back to JJ and pressed the folder against his chest. "If this is more trouble, take it away."

He held up his hands. "You have to hear me out."

Once in the kitchen she threw the paperwork on the table. "Let me guess, Ann is either trying to get me arrested or taking me to court."

JJ sat down and spread out his hand. "No."

Curious, Cora slid into a nearby chair. "Then what?"

JJ pointed to the dreaded folder. "That's Robert Hamilton Williams' will."

Her brows wrinkled and she asked in an uncertain tone, "What does my father's will have to do with me?"

JJ let out a huff of air. "A lot."

"How so?"

He picked up the folder and pulled out a stack of documents. "This has gone through probate and it landed on my desk about twenty minutes ago. After reading it, I came directly here."

"I don't understand. The man hated me."

JJ tilted his head. "Maybe, but he left every single thing he owned to Jack and made you the paid executor of the estate."

Cora slumped back and blinked several times before she could even think what to say. "But, I thought my mother would get his property."

JJ shook his head. "He didn't leave her a dime."

Cora licked her lips. "I don't want Jack to have his dirty money."

"The law took what they assumed was dirty, the rest he came by legally."

She lifted her chin and stared at JJ. "When was this will made?"

"The day Eleanor was murdered."

Tears filled her eyes at the thought of her beautiful sister dying and leaving Jack alone and unprotected. "Why?"

Again JJ shook his head. "I can't say. Maybe your mother can shed some light on the situation."

Her mother's cold face appeared in front of her. "Oh dear, she's not going to like this. She plans on having Father's money once released from prison." She looked at JJ. "How did he expect her to live?"

"Maybe he somehow suspected the truth and this was his way of paying her back for all the lies."

"I guess if he had any indication I was his real child, he would be angry enough to do something like this."

She hadn't touched the papers until now. With shaking hands, she looked at her father's powerful signature at the end of the document. "How much are we talking about?"

JJ rubbed his chin. "After talking to the lawyer who took care of your father's affairs, I'd say fifty thousand dollars."

She nearly fell out of the chair. "Are you kidding?"

"The house they lived in is rather extravagant. Wouldn't you say?"

It was absolutely lavish. "So, he didn't intend for Mother to stay there?"

"No, he clearly stipulated that she was to have nothing from the estate. The house and all the belonging were to be sold and the money put into Jack's trust."

Mentally numb, Cora leaned forward with her hands on her knees. She glanced at Jack, who lay sprawled on the floor with a comic book, oblivious that he'd suddenly become very rich. She desperately wanted to talk to Virgil. To get his advice, for him to help her with this task, and take all the madness go away.

"JJ, I thought all this was over when my father died." She took her cousin's hand. "I never cared for my father. I never wanted anything he ever had. I have a difficult time even giving it to Jack."

"You think about it for a few days. You don't have to do anything right away. But, eventually this matter will have to be settled, and the sooner the better."

"I'll talk to Virgil tonight."

JJ stood. "Fine, call me tomorrow." He glanced at the Christmas tree. "That's nice." He grinned.

When she followed his gaze, a chuckle escaped her lips. Tilting to the side slightly, the pathetic thing was only decorated as far up as the boys could reach and all the ornaments were in one area. "I promise this will get better."

JJ shook his head. "It's mighty big, but I'm sure your family will enjoy it."

As she walked him to the door, she remembered the Williams' servants who'd been so kind to her and Jack when she was released from prison. "Where are Naomi and Franklin?" She helped him on with his coat. "Are they still staying in St. Louis in my father's house?"

"No, they had to move in with her sister in Joplin. My guess is that's where they'll stay. They're both too old to get jobs."

She bit her lip. "Father left nothing for them after all their years of service?"

"Not a dime."

She glanced back at Jack, wondering what he'd think about the two people who'd put them on their feet once they arrived in Gibbs City, being thrown out on the street.

As JJ opened the door, Cora touched his arm. "How soon can we put our hands on some of that money?"

He looked surprised. "Immediately, I assume."

"And a certain amount belongs to me?"

"Yes, since you're a paid executor."

"Good, we're going to need it."

CHAPTER SIX

Virgil met David Batcher, the St. Louis police detective he'd worked with on Cora's case, at his precinct. The men shook hands and Virgil followed him to his desk in the crowded bull pen.

"I have the arrest warrants." He glanced over his shoulder. "You ready for this?"

"Yeah, those two sent a man named Harley Bremen to Gibbs City to kidnap Jack. Apparently they paid him fifteen hundred to take the job and promised another two grand when he delivered the boy. He claims he wasn't going to harm Jack, but he was carrying a loaded gun."

"Bastard." Batcher slipped on his coat. "We'll run that name before you leave."

"I'm keeping him in my county considering he doesn't look too good right now." Virgil grinned. "He tripped."

Batcher smiled and slapped Virgil on the back. "Good man. I hope you messed him up good. The crime happened there so he's yours legally."

"And I plan to keep him as far away from his attorney as I can. I have a feeling the Martins have assured him if he runs into trouble they have help available."

Virgil continued, "He asked for a lawyer too soon. The average bad guy, unless he makes a habit of needing legal counsel, doesn't have a lawyer they can reach out to. He did."

"Well, he's where he belongs," Batcher said. "Let's hope the judge throws the book at him."

They left the office as nightfall swept over the bustling city. With the holidays right around the corner, the streets were crowded with shoppers and children marveling at the department store window displays. A Santa stood on the corner ringing a bell, and multicolored lights were strung around the whole downtown area.

Batcher blew into his hands. "Your family ready for Christmas?"

Virgil thought of the poor excuse of a tree standing in their living room. He'd have to find a replacement. One that was definitely smaller and more evenly branched. As Christmas drew closer, he realized he didn't have time to deal with this kind of meanness.

"No, it's not been the heart-warming, home, hearth, and candy cane event I had envisioned."

Batcher opened the door to his standard issue unmarked car and slid inside. Virgil jumped in beside him.

"With everything you were put through recently, I don't know how you keep anything together. My God, man. For a small town, Gibbs City has had its share of troubles."

Virgil leaned back. "You're telling me. And with Cora expecting, there is so much to do."

Batcher slapped him on the arm. "You lucky dog. How many men have what you've got? A nice wife, a son, and a new baby on the way."

Virgil looked at him and grinned. "You're not doing so badly yourself. You have two kids and a beautiful wife, too."

"I do, and I take the time to thank God every day. On the way to work I pray that I'll make it back home to them that evening."

"We all do."

"There are a couple of uniforms meeting us at the Martin house should we need them."

"Good idea."

They pulled into the exclusive neighborhood of the rich in name and status. Virgil had been there before. The home belonging to the Martins was huge with a full staff of servants, and in the summer, the lawn looked more like a recently vacuumed rug than grass.

Now, everything was covered in snow and the house was richly decorated without appearing gaudy. Candles in every window and smoke came from the four tall chimneys. Those driving by could easily assume a normal, loving family lived inside. Nothing could be further from the truth.

"Well," Batcher said. "It looks like we're going to ruin their holidays."

"Yeah, I'm kind of looking forward to that part."

"You know they'll have a lawyer waiting at the station before we get them there."

"I'm sure they've informed the servants who to call. But we're talking serious charges now."

"And with a signed confession, this could be over in no time."

Virgil looked at Batcher and shook his head. "You honestly think that?"

Batcher ducked his head. "No, not in your case."

He and the detective left the car at the same time and walked up the sidewalk that led to the double front doors. A quick knock had a colored maid at the door before Batcher could take the warrant out of his pocket.

"Are Ann and Dan Martin home?"

"Yes, sir." She opened the door wider. "Who should I say is calling?"

"The St. Louis Police Department."

Fear shone in her eyes before the woman hurried away. While the maid had been quick, Ann and Dan kept them waiting to the point Virgil was ready to storm the place. No doubt they were getting their stories straight. They had to suspect that Bremen was in custody or the police wouldn't be standing at their door.

Mrs. Martin came into the room, meticulously dressed in a red sheath designer dress, high heels and a colorful scarf around her neck. She also had a glass of liquor in her left hand and gold chains dangled from her wrists. Seeing Virgil, her eyes widened and her brows lifted. The smile on her face stiffened, all in an effort not to reveal her surprise. "What's the meaning of this?" she asked politely.

Dan came and stood behind his mother, belligerently glaring at Virgil over her shoulder. He also looked ready to go out for the evening.

"We're here to arrest the two of you," Batcher said in a professional tone. Waving the warrant, he smiled. "I have the necessary papers to take you to the precinct and book you on accessory to an attempted kidnapping."

Virgil put his hands in his pockets and rocked back on his heels. "Mr. Bremen failed. Jack's safe and sound at home with Cora and your man is in jail."

Ann turned to her son. "Do we know anyone by the name of Bremen?"

"Absolutely not."

"He certainly knows you. Right now, it's all up to a judge," Batcher said. "But be advised Bremen has signed a confession."

Ann lifted her chin and sniffed as if she smelled something foul. "I think you're insane. My son and I have no idea what you're talking about." She reached over and took her clutch purse from the table. "Now if you'll excuse us, we've been invited to the Governor's Ball. It wouldn't be wise for you to detain us."

Batcher took his handcuffs out of his pocket and held them up. "Judge's orders."

Virgil did exactly as Batcher, only his grin was so big, his face hurt. "I'll take Dan, you take her."

Batcher pulled Ann aside and spun her around to put the shackles on while Virgil reached for Dan. He tried to squirm out of Virgil's grasp. Jerking Dan closer, Virgil placed his face inches from Dan's and hissed, "Please give me a reason to stomp you into the ground."

Dan reared back, his eyes darting around in fear. "Don't you dare lay a hand on me. If you do, I'll have your badge. Our attorney will bury you."

Virgil chuckled. "Didn't you try that once before?" He leaned closer. "Little boy."

With the two in the backseat screaming like banshees, the threats, curse words and accusations didn't stop until they reached the police station.

Two uniforms escorted the prisoners into the precinct, while Virgil and Batcher took a breather outside. The detective rubbed his forehead. "I have a headache. I wanted to stop and bash their heads together."

"Me too," Virgil said. "But we have to go by the book on this one. Besides, no one knows what Ann has up her sleeve. She's a cunning bitch who's out for blood."

"I can't help but wonder why the hell they just don't leave you and your family alone. I figured with the trial all this would end." Batcher tugged his coat tighter against the harsh weather. "Trying to kidnap a child is serious business."

"I know, and I'm as confused as you. Maybe they're the type of people who just can't let go and get on with their lives."

Batcher shrugged and opened the precinct door. "Who knows anymore?"

Ann and Dan had been put into separate interviewing rooms. "Let's talk to the kid. He's scared of his own shadow," Batcher suggested. "I don't think his heart is in this. Mama's running this show."

"Good idea. Let's leave the mastermind for later."

CHAPTER SEVEN

Earl came over just as Cora put dinner on the table. He hung his coat and made his way to Jack. "After dinner, take all that stuff off the tree. I had Carl cut down another one that will fit in the house."

Jack jumped up. "But this is the tree me and Dad cut down. It's special."

"Course it is, but it's also bigger than the house and its branches are too bare. Besides, we don't have enough stuff to cover the monstrosity. We'll put that in the backyard and you kids can play with it, but the other one will fit better."

Not looking too happy with the situation, Jack said, "Aw okay." He slowly dragged his feet as he walked toward the table. "Dad's going to be real disappointed."

"No, he won't, because we're putting up the new tree and decorating it tonight. He'll be surprised when he gets home and sees it."

Jack finally smiled, but dropped the expression when he glanced at the bedraggled tree. "It does look kind of sad, doesn't it?"

"It's not that, Jack," Earl explained. "It's just too darn big. And with Christmas only three days away, we have to get it ready for Santa."

Jack rubbed his hands together. "I can hardly wait."

"Well, you know he's keeping a really close eye on all the little boys and girls this time of year. He has a good list and a naughty list." Earl helped Jack onto his chair. "You don't want to end up on the wrong list."

"He can ask Mom. I've been really good, lately."

Earl sat at the table and Cora relaxed as the two bantered back and forth. Hand resting on her stomach, she smiled as she thought of all the wonderful people who made up the town of Gibbs City. Glancing at Earl, she realized he was one of the very best.

She prayed that everything would go smoothly in St. Louis and Virgil could finally get Ann and Dan to realize she and Virgil weren't giving up Jack. Not for the world.

Serving the food, Earl looked at her. "You okay, Missy?"

She forced a smile. "I always miss Virgil when he's away from home. I can't help but worry."

"Well, ain't no need for that. That man's been able to take care of himself since he was old enough to walk. You don't grow up with the two rough and rowdy brothers like he had and not be able to give as good as you got."

Her heart squeezed. "It's sad that he lost them in the war."

Earl held up his hand. "Now, let's don't get into all that. Before you know it, you'll be crying all over the place and Jack will get upset and join you."

She grinned. The old softy couldn't stand to see her cry without tearing up himself. "Yes, this is a festive time. And I'm glad we're decorating the tree tonight. It would be sad if Santa came to drop off the presents and there wasn't any place to put them."

"I keep wondering how a fat man like him is going to get down the chimney."

"Magic," Earl said, matter-of-factly. "Just like everything else about the man."

Jack stabbed a green bean and studied it carefully. "What if Santa misses my house?"

"Oh, don't you worry about that. He'll make a stop here."

Cora took a sip of coffee. "Jack, you need to decide what you're going to do about the school play."

"Don't be in no hurry," Earl said. "Tomorrow afternoon the board's meeting to get to the bottom of why Jack, Ronnie and Tommy were left out."

Cora shook her head. "I like Miss Potter." She looked at her son. "I find it hard to believe she's been mistreating any of the children, especially Ronnie."

Jack put his fork down and looked at the two of them, his face serious and his eyes narrowed. "Mom, Uncle Earl, I don't want to be no trouble. But Miss Potter is real nice to us in front of you, but when you leave, she's mean."

Cora leaned closer. "How?"

"She's always yelling, and screaming at us for everything. She shoves us around, yanks all the kids by their collars. Stuff like that."

"But you used to like her, Jack. When we first came here you were fond of Miss Potter."

"I was." Jack shrugged. "Then she changed."

Cora and Earl shared a curious glance as the little boy went back to eating his dinner.

Earl winked. "We'll get to the bottom of it."

As Cora pulled a chocolate cake from the pie chest, Jack left the table for his radio program. "As soon as Superman is over, I'll get busy, okay, Uncle Earl?"

"That's fine, Son."

While Earl cut the cake, she poured fresh coffee for them and a glass of milk for Jack. "Did you hear Granny Riley protected the boys earlier today?"

"I did, and I stopped by to thank her and see how she was doing." Earl looked away. "Sophia's always been a powerfully strong woman. Gave her husband a run for his money, all right. But she's decent folks and I've always considered her a friend."

"Aren't you two around the same age?"

He thought for a minute. "I think so. She and Wanda knew each other pretty well. I remember it being said that they were about the same age."

"I have a lot to do. But tonight I'm baking a Christmas cake and taking it to her tomorrow."

"Now what on earth is a Christmas cake?"

"I've only made one, but they're delicious."

"Then don't you think maybe you should make two?" He smiled and raised his eyebrows.

"I probably should." Cora sat down. "Does she spend the holidays with Carl and his family?"

"Oh yeah. They're all really close. That woman almost worried herself to death while Carl was away fighting the war. I never seen anything like it."

"Is he her only child?"

"No, she has a daughter, Carolyn, in Carthage. Carolyn comes by every week to check on her mother and they'll be there Christmas Day."

She put her hand on his and looked in his eyes. "I want to discuss something rather troubling."

Alarm and concern filled his eyes. "The baby?"

"No, she's fine."

"Then what?"

"JJ came by today. It seems my father left all his money to Jack in an estate that I'm in control of."

Earl leaned back, his mouth open, his gaze disbelieving. "Does he have any money after the District Attorney got done with him?"

"Almost fifty thousand dollars."

Earl whistled. "That's a lot of money." He glanced at Jack who sat on the couch with Pal on his lap. "That's a powerful amount. I guess we don't have to worry about paying for his college."

"You're right," Cora replied. "But there are a few things I'd like to do with some of the money."

"Exactly what do you have in mind?"

She smiled. "You'll see."

CHAPTER EIGHT

Virgil and Batcher opened the door to Dan's room and looked at the pathetic bastard. The little weasel was enough to turn Virgil's stomach. Jack couldn't possibly belong to that man.

Batcher threw a folder on the table. Inside was a copy of Bremen's confession. Dan didn't know that, but he'd soon find out. If they could make the charges stick, the Martin family would be out of their lives forever.

Batcher put his palms on the table and leaned down. "Harley Bremen said you and your mother gave him fifteen hundred dollars to kidnap Jack Martin. He claims when he handed over the kid, he was promised another two grand."

"That's a lie," Dan said as perspiration gathered on his forehead. "How can a father kidnap his own son?"

Virgil glared at the man. "You don't have a son."

"Jack belongs to me."

Virgil leaned down. "You think so? How many nights have you sat up with him while he was sick? Held his hand at the dentist while he got a tooth pulled? Tucked him into bed? Fallen to your knees every night and prayed that he will always be safe?" Virgil straightened. "That's what a real dad does."

"Go to hell."

"We have you now, Martin," Batcher said. "And your daddy isn't here to help you out."

"I swear I don't even know the man."

"Sure you do," Virgil accused. "He's the one you hired."

Dan leaned back and hooked his arm over the back of the chair.

"You're crazy. You think some judge is going to take the word of a man with a record as long as your arm, over mine?"

Virgil leaned against the wall. "I didn't say he had a record. We haven't even investigated him yet." Virgil smiled and glanced at Batcher. "But thanks for the information."

Dan jumped to his feet, only for Batcher to shove him back down. "Don't make me handcuff you."

"I'm only assuming," he shouted. "What other kind of person would kidnap a kid?"

Virgil glared up and down at the sorry excuse for a man. "A man dressed in a tux with a grudge to settle, perhaps?"

"I was here. You can't pin anything on me."

"Newsflash," Batcher said. "We already have."

They left the room and watched through the one-way glass as Dan paced restlessly. "That's one guilty SOB there," Virgil said. "And I hope he spends the rest of his life in jail."

Virgil thumbed over his shoulder. "Let's see what she has to say."

Batcher opened the door and Ann Martin crossed her arms and turned away. "I have nothing to say."

"You don't have to," Virgil said. "Your son did enough talking for both of you."

She glared at Virgil. "I swear, if it's the last thing on this earth I do, I'm going to make you pay for this."

He smiled. "I'm proud to hear you say that, Ann. The end might be closer than you think."

The door opened and a man in a rumpled black suit came in with droopy eyes, looking like he'd just crawled out of bed. "My client has nothing to say, gentlemen. I suggest you save your breath."

The St. Louis District Attorney John Osborn walked into the room. "All the judges are out for the holidays. Looks like your clients are going to spend that time behind bars."

The lawyer huffed. "We'll see about that. I have a few favors to call in."

John leaned his shoulder on the doorframe and crossed his ankles. "You don't anymore. Judge Ferris and Judge Coleman are under indictment. They won't be releasing anyone."

The lawyer looked like he'd swallowed his tongue. "Are you serious?"

"Yes, sir." He straightened and slid his hands in his pockets. "I heard that about two hours ago."

The lawyer pointed to Virgil and Batcher. "Then how did they get a warrant?"

John smiled. "I called in a few favors too. Fortunately, the judges I deal with are honest."

That made the long trip to St. Louis well worth the drive to Virgil.

Sometimes the good guys win.

Ann rose angrily, knocking her chair over with a crash. Her face flushed with anger and utter disbelief, she said, "Do you mean to say that my son and I will be in jail for Christmas?"

Virgil chuckled then slapped Batcher on the shoulder. "This makes you believe in Santa Claus, doesn't it?"

An officer came in and handcuffed a struggling Ann Martin. As he escorted her to the door, Virgil watched Dan being led from the opposite room.

Virgil gratefully reached to shake John Osborn's hand. "Thank you. You have no idea the peace of mind you just gave my family."

The District Attorney grinned slyly. "Maybe a certain judge in Gibbs City gave me a little assistance."

"Judge Garner?"

John walked away without confirming Virgil's suspicion. He turned to Batcher. "I don't know about you, but I'm starving. My wife fixed me lunch, but when I stopped for gas I saw a family whose car had broken down. Their kids needed the food more than I did."

Batcher put his arm around him and grinned. "You're a good guy, Carter, but you sure are a sucker for kids."

CHAPTER NINE

Cora had been dozing in the chair when the phone rang. Startled, she jumped then grabbed the handset. "Virgil?"

"Hi, sweetheart. Is everything okay?"

She clasped both hands around the receiver to feel closer to him. "We're fine," she said, relieved to hear the sound of his voice. "Did you arrest them?"

"Yes, they're locked up at least until after the holidays. All the judges are out for Christmas break."

Fearful, Cora placed her shaking hands on her stomach. "I'm sure they were angry to learn that."

His deep chuckle carried from the phone to warm her body. She missed him so much. Although they'd remained busy, her thoughts were never far from her husband's safety.

"They were not happy."

"Good, I'm glad Jack is safe," Cora said. "Did you learn why they wanted to kidnap Jack?"

"No, not directly, however, Dan said a father can't be accused of kidnapping his own son."

"Don't you find it strange that they didn't want Jack when I was in prison, but now that I'm out and we're happy, they are doing everything possible to gain custody of him?"

"That hasn't escaped my notice, Cora. There is something going on we know nothing about."

"What are we going to do?"

"I'm going to do a lot of investigating between now and the time they go to trial."

"I know you'll get to the bottom of this mess."

"For now, Jack is safe."

"I'm glad," she said. But it's so late. Are you just now getting to the hotel?"

"Yes, Batcher and I had dinner and talked for a while."

"I'm glad you have someone you can share your thoughts with. It has to be difficult on you to do what you do and rarely be able to discuss anything."

"I'm kind of used to it."

She bit her bottom lip and wondered if she should talk to Virgil on the phone or wait until tomorrow when he returned home. Deciding she had to move quickly, she said, "While you've been away a few things have happened."

"What?" A sense of dread deepened his voice. "What's wrong?"

"Nothing awful, but there are a few things we need to discuss."

"Okay, tell me."

"Are you sure you're not too tired?"

"Cora, tell me what the hell is going on. Is it the baby?"

"Virgil, no," she hushed. "It's not bad."

"I'm sorry. It's been a long day. I'm listening."

"First, Earl had Ethan drag out the tree you and Jack cut down. Carl replaced it with a much nicer one."

"Well, I don't think the tree was that bad." The sadness in Virgil's voice slowed his speech.

"It was pretty big."

"I could've trimmed it a little."

"Virgil, half the branches were gone and those left on the tree were already dried out," she carefully pointed out.

"Okay." He let out a deep sigh. "So we have a different tree."

"Earl, Jack and I decorated it tonight. We're just waiting for you to put the star on top." She looked around at the red ribbon taped to the wall in the living room, several of Jack's Christmas drawings, ornamental knick-knacks scattered around the house, and a beautifully decorated tree. "It's quite festive. I'm sure you'll love it."

"If you're happy, so am I. Now, what's the reason we're talking at this hour?"

"JJ came by this afternoon and informed me that my father left everything he owned to Jack. He put it in an estate that I control. And before you ask, it's almost fifty thousand dollars."

Surprise tinged his voice. "He had that kind of money left?"

"According to JJ, this is all legal money."

"Huh, what made him do that I wonder."

"He didn't leave my mother a thing. I'm tempted to contact her and find out why."

"You might be able to call her during the holidays."

"But, how do I tell her that she has no place to live and no money to call her own?"

"You have ten years to figure that out."

"There are a few things I'd like to do with a very small amount of the money."

"Careful, honey. That doesn't belong to you."

"I know, but I am a paid executor." She wrinkled her nose. "Not that I want the money for me."

"You're not thinking about buying a bigger house are you?"

"No, of course not. This money will be put aside for Jack's college and then a good start afterwards."

"I've always wanted him to be able to attend college. One day a person won't be able to get a good job without a degree."

Relieved she'd put it all out there, Cora let out a deep breath. "That wasn't so bad."

"I'm glad you feel better. Now what do you want to spend some of the money on."

"I don't want to tell you. But I want you to say it's okay if I do."

"As long as you don't spend a dime on something for me. I have everything I ever dreamed of, Cora. I wake up every day feeling blessed."

"I know, I do too."

"If you promise me that whatever you want to do won't interfere with our lives then I think you should do what you feel in your heart."

She gripped the phone tighter and smiled. "I love you."

"I love you too, darling. I can't wait to get home tomorrow."

"Oh, well, you have a school board meeting in the afternoon."

"So soon?"

"That's what Earl said at dinner."

"I just don't understand all this. I can't imagine what turned Ruth from a wonderful, caring young lady into an unkind teacher."

"Maybe you'll find out tomorrow. But I don't want Jack dragged into this."

"No, I'll recount what he said. I'll talk to him before I go to the meeting."

"Just so you know, Ethan came by tonight and said that Harley Bremen was taken to the hospital in Carthage and they'll keep him until his arraignment."

"That sounds bad."

"He has several broken ribs, broken jaw, broken nose and a broken hand. Please tell me you didn't do that."

"I didn't do *all* of it."

As a physician, she was disturbed that the man she loved could have beaten a prisoner. As Jack's mom, she wished Virgil had shot the man who'd tried to harm her son. "You're horrible."

"Hey, he came after our son, he's lucky I didn't blow his brains out."

"Okay, okay. I won't say another word about it. But the school play is tomorrow night and Jack is standing firm with his friends. They all refuse to be elves."

Virgil chuckled. "I expected that."

She smiled. "Just like the Three Musketeers. They'll stick together through thick and thin."

He yawned. "That's good in a way. A man needs good friends."

"Oh, one more thing. After the school's play, Maggie, Susan and I have to go to Arthur's house to wrap presents for the tree ceremony."

"We're going to be busy."

"Also, we have some wrapping of our own to do." The phone went quiet. She waited, but Virgil didn't say anything. "Are you there?"

"Yeah, I'm going to need some time before Christmas to shop. With so much going on, I haven't bought you a single thing."

Placing her hand on her stomach, she said, "You gave me our little baby."

"Well." He lowered his voice. "That was my pleasure."

Heat rushed to her cheeks. "I'll see you tomorrow. I love you. Be careful."

"I love you too, sweetheart. I'm be there as soon as I can."

CHAPTER TEN

Virgil arrived home the next day to a winter wonderland in his own home. The place looked like a department store window. After removing his coat, he knelt down as Jack ran toward him. "Dad, you're back." Jack threw his arms around Virgil's neck and showed him a gapped-toothed grin.

"Yes, I am." Shoving back his Stetson, he looked around. "I see you've been busy."

"Mom says it's way over the moon, but I like it. Don't you?"

After petting Pal, Virgil stood and looked at Cora standing near the kitchen sink.

"I warned you," she said. "Earl and Jack got a little carried away."

"Dad." Jack tugged at his pant leg. "Santa will be sure to find our house now, won't he?"

Virgil chuckled. "How on earth could he miss it?"

Jack sobered. "Do you like the tree? You have to put the star on top. Mom said it's going to be our Christmas tra...tradiction."

"*Tradition*." Virgil took the star. Yeah, it's a perfect fit. Let's take care of that tradition, right now. But I'll need a little help." Reaching down, he handed Jack the star and swung him up to place the star on the top. It was slightly crooked, but they thought it was beautiful.

Setting Jack on his feet, he watched as the boy tilted his head and frowned. "It's pretty, but it's not mine and yours."

He ruffled Jack's hair. "That's because we're not the best judge of trees while they're still in the woods. We'll do better next year."

Jack's smile returned. "Yeah, we'll get better."

Cora walked over, put her arms around him and kissed him on the mouth. He'd missed her touch, even for one night. Until last night he'd never realized how empty a bed could feel. Tonight, he'd have her snuggled up next to him and that brought a smile to his face.

"Lunch is ready," she said. "Then I think you'll just have time to get to the school board meeting."

"Lucky me," Virgil mumbled. "After a long drive that's exactly what I want to do."

"I know," Cora said. "But we need to make sure Miss Potter is the best person to teach our children."

"I agree." Virgil put his bag away then filled the empty thermos with water to soak. He took his seat at the table and reached for a sandwich. "I only had coffee this morning. I'm starving. I could eat a bear."

Jack smiled. "Mom fixed my special pancakes."

Virgil stopped as he brought the sandwich to his mouth. "She did?" He took a bite and chewed. "That means I missed out on a big stack of flapjacks."

"You sure did," Jack gloated.

Virgil placed his sandwich on the plate and reached for his drink with a frown. "I don't rightly think that's fair." He leaned over and kissed Cora. "Maybe I can have them tomorrow?"

She gave him a sassy smile. "Maybe. I did save you a piece of chocolate cake for later."

Just as Virgil drained the last bit of coffee from his cup, Earl came in wearing his Sunday best. "You ready for the meeting?"

"I'm just finishing lunch."

"You barely made it back in time." He glanced at Jack. "Did you take care of that matter in St. Louis?"

"All locked up."

Earl smiled. "Good, that's what I like to hear."

A knock sounded at the door, just as Jack ran out the back to go play with Tommy. Now that Bremen and the two in St. Louis were behind bars, Cora and Virgil were comfortable letting Jack leave the house.

Virgil went to the front door and found Ruth Potter standing there with tears in her eyes. "I've come to give you my resignation."

Cora joined them and said, "Please, come inside."

"There's no reason for that, Miss Potter," Virgil said. "We can all come to an agreement."

"No," she said loudly. "There's no fix for this."

Cora took her by the hand and led her to the couch and encouraged her to sit. "I can't imagine what has you so upset." She looked at Earl. "But surely it can be made right."

"Cora's telling the truth," Earl said. "I don't know what's going on but we'll discuss it at the meeting."

"I'm not going to the meeting. I refuse to discuss anything this personal with the board."

Cora pulled her closer, while Virgil sat on the edge of a nearby chair. "What's so personal that you'd give up teaching? You love your job."

Brushing away angry tears, Ruth said, "Not anymore. I can hardly stand to walk into that building."

"Why?" Earl asked. "What's there that has you so fired up?"

Ruth glanced at Earl then ducked her head. "Nothing we can talk about."

Virgil leaned forward, his elbows on his thighs. "Ruth, you have to tell us what's going on. Is this a matter for the law?"

Ruth chewed her bottom lip. "I don't know."

Earl sat on the arm of the couch. "That means it is."

Putting her arm around the young woman's shoulders, Cora said, "You can trust us. Whatever you say in this house goes no further."

Virgil grew uncomfortable as Ruth cried her eyes out. He'd never seen a woman so distraught. Her eyes were red and swollen, and she looked as though she hadn't slept in days. What on earth could be going on to bring on such heartache?

Cora placed Ruth's head on her shoulder and patted her back. She gave him a questioning glance, but he could only shrug. He had no idea what this was about. Virgil took out his watch and checked the time. Arthur, Judge Garner and Carl would be waiting for them at the community hall.

Cora said, "Why are you so upset you want to resign? That doesn't make sense."

"I can't go back there anymore."

Cora took her by the shoulder and stared into her eyes. "Tell us why."

"Because of him." She wiped away fresh tears. "I can't let him continue to do this to me."

"Who?" Virgil asked. "Is someone hurting you?"

"Not unless you consider words."

Still holding Ruth's hands, Cora asked, "Is someone blackmailing you? Forcing you to do things against your will?"

She covered her face with the lacy handkerchief and bawled. "Yes."

Virgil and Cora shared a familiar glance.

"And you said this person is a man?" Virgil asked.

"Yes."

Giving Miss Potter a gentle shake, Cora encouraged her to raise her head. Earl fidgeted uncomfortably and handed the woman his large white handkerchief.

"If someone is holding something over your head, we don't tolerate that," Earl said. "You tell us because we have the right to know."

"If I tell you then you'll fire me."

"Well," Earl said. "You were going to resign anyway. Maybe if we know what's happening we can solve the whole mess."

Ruth blew her nose and looked at Cora. "I'm in a lot of trouble."

"How," Cora asked. "Who's causing you so much distress?"

"The Principal, Paul Russell."

That certainly surprised Virgil. He'd always thought Paul was a nice man. He'd been a good administrator, and as far as Virgil knew, the other two teachers liked him. "Is he threatening you, Miss Potter?"

She nodded.

"How?"

She twisted the hankie in her lap so tightly, Virgil feared it would tear. "He knows about my past."

"What about it?"

"Reverend Washburn and I knew each other years ago." She glanced at Virgil. "Very well."

"Nothing wrong with that."

"If something unethical happened between us there would be."

Earl stood and began pacing. They knew what she was talking about now and it made him uncomfortable.

Finally Earl stopped and glanced down at Ruth. "How long ago was this?"

"Almost six years."

"You weren't a school teacher then and I doubt Washburn was a preacher."

Silence roamed through the house like an unwanted visitor.

"You didn't just have an affair," Cora said. "There's more."

"This all happened when Daniel and I were young. I thought we were going to get married as soon as we finished school. But, without a word, he went off to seminary school."

"You didn't know he planned to leave?" Cora asked.

"We'd talked a little about him doing that. I thought someday he might join the ministry, except I thought I would be with him."

Virgil moved closer. "And Principal Russell has been holding that information over your head?"

"Yes,"

"What's he threatening to do?"

"He said he would tell the whole town, and mine and Daniel's lives would be ruined forever."

"Or..." Cora asked.

"I had to agree to meet him at the motel outside of town twice a week."

"Have you done that?" Virgil asked. Nothing made him madder than a man manipulating a woman for sex. Dammit, if a woman said no, she meant no.

"Not yet." Her gaze dropped to her lap again. "I've been stalling and putting him off. Lately, he's become very physical. He's started slapping me, grabbing my breasts, trying to pin me in corners."

Her face crumpled. "It's just so horrible. That's why I've been so unkind with the children. I'm so frightened and frustrated. I had no place to turn."

Virgil took Ruth's hand. "You know you can always come to me. I'd never knowingly allow this to happen in my town."

"I didn't want you to think badly of me. It just horrified me to death to think that the people of Gibbs City would turn against me."

"They won't," Cora assured her. "How can they?"

"Cora's right," Earl said. "All this happened a long time ago and you shouldn't be made to pay for it the rest of your life."

"And don't worry," Virgil said. "We'll take care of the principal."

"But, you don't understand," Ruth said.

"Understand what?" Cora asked.

"I had a child out of wedlock. A little girl. She lives with my sister in Joplin." Ruth wiped her face. "Daniel didn't know that I was expecting Sally when he went away."

Virgil stood. "That changes everything."

CHAPTER ELEVEN

Cora was stunned. Ruth had an illegitimate child that she'd kept hidden for years. How in the world had she managed to pull that off? After giving the idea some thought, Cora realized Ruth had managed the same way her Aunt Rose and JJ's father had. Cora squeezed Ruth's hand. "And Reverend Washburn doesn't know?"

She looked scared out of her wits. "No." She looked away. "I couldn't ruin his future. Besides, I didn't want him to think he had to marry me."

"I can understand that, but he has a right to know."

She clutched Cora hands. "No, he doesn't. When he went away, I never heard from him again. I learned later that he had a congregation and was well respected. He didn't need me or Sally."

"That's your opinion," Cora said, "You never gave Daniel a choice."

"I don't want him to know."

Earl rubbed his hands over his face. "Ruth, you can't be a teacher and have a child with no husband."

"Why not?" She stiffened. "I'm good at my job." She dropped her gaze. "As long as I'm not being chased by a man demanding sexual favors."

"The parents of Gibbs City won't allow it," Virgil said. "I think it's wrong as wrong can be, but people have small minds. It would be really tough for you to make it through this and keep your job."

"Can't you keep Mr. Russell from spreading gossip about me?"

"If you're asking if I can keep your secret hidden, the answer is no. He has the right to speak his mind. I can encourage him to do the right thing by mentioning that maybe his wife could get wind of his behavior. But that's no guarantee."

Cora's heart went out to the young school teacher. The reverend would probably be unscathed and able to continue being their minister, but Ruth would have to pay the price for their indiscretions.

"But, maybe it will work," Cora said.

Earl cleared his throat. "No it won't. Paul Russell is going to be fired. We can't have a man treating one of our teachers like that. Once that's done, he might not be so willing to keep his mouth shut."

Ruth sighed. "So, I might as well resign and leave town."

Cora looked at Ruth. "Do you plan to tell the reverend about Sally?"

"No, he doesn't need that. He's just started here in Gibbs City. That could ruin everything for him."

Earl harrumphed. "It could make him a better man, too."

Virgil put his hand on Earl's shoulder and led him into the kitchen. Soon their heads were together and both talking rapidly, but quietly. Cora wondered what they were up to.

Virgil approached them. "Cora, can you come with us to the meeting?"

"We think," Earl said, "that Ruth needs a woman handy for moral support."

"If Maggie agrees to watch Jack."

Cora called Maggie then they all left for the community hall. Inside, Arthur the judge, Carl, two other teachers and Principal Russell waited. The mayor was in the hospital with pneumonia. Earl immediately dismissed the teachers who taught the older children.

Cora took a seat next to Ruth and grasped her hand. Virgil sat beside her. When their eyes met, they shared a weary smile.

Standing in for the mayor, Arthur walked to the front of the room where all town hall, council and school board meetings were held.

Cora stole a glance at Principal Russell, who sat smugly at the end of the row of chairs. He probably figured Ruth would never tell anyone what he'd tried to make her do. Little did he know.

"Thank you for being here. Miss Carter, you're not a member of the board, but you may remain at the request of Miss Potter."

"Thank you," Cora muttered.

"We're here to discuss recent allegations that Miss Potter has been treating certain children under her care with malice. She has not harmed a child, but she's given certain students reason to complain."

Paul Russell stood. He was a man with a wide waistline, short legs, and thinning hair. He looked at least fifty and had a double chin. "I think those matters should've been brought to my attention and I would've easily dealt with them."

Arthur shot him a stern glance. "Because the school play is tonight, and that is the matter to be discussed, Earl decided to handle the situation immediately."

Paul pointed at Earl. "Well, who's he to decide such things? I'm the principal and I'm her supervisor. This should wait until after the holidays."

Earl stood. "The board decided on today, and we're your supervisors."

Paul staggered backwards as if stuck. "How dare you speak to me in that tone? I've been the principal around here for fifteen years."

Arthur slammed down the gavel. "Let's get this over with. Miss Potter, what do you have to say about these claims?"

Arthur took his seat and Ruth stepped to the front of the room. "I'm guilty." Voices rumbled around the room. "I was rude like the children claimed."

The judge spoke up. "Ruth, do you have a reason for this new behavior? I've always considered you a good teacher who cared deeply for the children of Gibbs City."

"I do," she proclaimed. "I love my job."

"So, what changed?" Arthur asked.

Ruth pointed to Paul Russell. "He did."

Mouth open wide enough to fit a pie in, the principal scrambled for words. "I...I...She's lying."

Carl looked at the principal. "She hasn't said anything yet, Mr. Russell."

"Just how has he changed?" the judge asked. "In what way?"

"He's made inappropriate demands of me and tried to force me into an affair." Her face red as the Santa costume in the corner, she continued, "He threatened to expose something in my past if I didn't have *relations* with him."

A gasp circled the room.

"That's a lie. She's been coming on to me. How dare she say something like that? I'm a married man." He jumped to his feet. "She has a kid by the reverend and they were never married."

"So," Earl asked, "is that what you threatened her with?"

"No," the principal shouted. "I did not."

"If you knew this," the judge asked, "why haven't you brought it to the board's attention?"

"I...I...She begged me not to."

Arthur stood. "Cora, can you take Miss Potter into the hallway? Virgil will come and get you when we've finished our discussion."

"Of course," Cora replied, reaching for Ruth's hand. Cora stood. "I'd like to say something, if I may."

Arthur nodded.

"There are times in everyone's life when things don't go as planned and in the midst of that, sometimes a person becomes a victim. That's what happened to Miss Potter. She made a mistake years ago that has now came back to haunt her. But, I ask you," Cora looked into the eyes of every man there. "Please consider Ruth as your sister, or your own daughter. And remember, we've all lived life. That means given the opportunity, there are several things we'd change."

"Is there anything else you want to say, Miss Potter?" Carl asked. "My youngest is quite fond of you, and I'd hate to see you leave us."

"I'm sorry, but what he says is true, Mr. Riley. I can't deny it."

Cora and Ruth left the room and closed the door quietly behind them. Ruth was so upset she looked pale and weak with her head lowered. "What a terrible time of the year for this to be happening."

Cora put her arm around her. "I understand. Sometimes life can be very difficult."

"How will I take care of my daughter?" She waved her hand at the door. "And when they're done, Daniel is going to know that I was pregnant when he left."

Cora stood in front of Ruth, and placed her palms on each side of the young woman's face. "Listen to me, Ruth. A man has a right to know he's a father. Even if he doesn't want to claim the child or if he wants to deny it's his. He still needs to know."

"I'm sure you're right, Cora. You probably think I've been very selfish."

"No," Cora said. "I, of all people, know how hard it is to live in peace."

In a few minutes, Virgil came out and asked them to return to the meeting. The somber faces of the men gathered in the room didn't lift her spirits as Cora took her seat and folded her hands on her lap. Ruth bit her lips.

Carl stepped to the front of the room. "We've decided that Mr. Russell is fired and cannot apply for school jobs in any nearby towns. He's agreed to be discreet as long this board is."

Cora glanced over at an angry Paul Russell, who had his arms crossed tightly around his body, gazing straight ahead.

That surprised Cora. Letting him off so easily didn't sit well with her and she wished the board would've charged him for his conduct toward Ruth.

Arthur stood, and looked at the ex-principal. "You are to leave now, Paul. Our suggestion is to find another town to live in."

They watched as the self-righteous principal left the room without looking back. Ruth let out a loud gasp. Cora thought the teacher would be the next one asked to leave. She glanced at Virgil for any indication as to the final verdict, but his features betrayed nothing.

"Miss Potter, this assembly has decided that you are to continue as the school teacher until the end of the year. At that time we ask that you either marry the father of your child or resign."

There was a moment of relief on Miss Potter's face, only to quickly be replaced with doubt and distress. It must have been difficult for her to consider facing the father of her child after all this time.

The teacher stood. "Thank you all very much. I promise to be the best teacher Gibbs City has ever had for the rest of my employment."

The board meeting was adjourned and Cora took Virgil by the hand. "I think that went rather nicely. At least Ruth doesn't have to get out of town."

"Not right now, but the day will come."

Squeezing his hand, Cora asked, "Where did the idea of her marrying Reverend Washburn come in?"

Virgil smiled down at her. "You and I of all people should be aware no one knows when love will come knocking. She needs to give the man a chance."

Laughing, Cora glanced at the gaily decorated town all lit up for Christmas. "Were you men playing Cupid?"

"I repeat, one never knows."

"I know we have to get home and convince a certain young man that he needs to change his mind about being in the school play."

"That's not going to be easy."

Swinging their arms, and humming a tune, Cora watched the bustling Christmas shoppers. "Being a parent never is."

CHAPTER TWELVE

Virgil went to get Jack and asked Tommy to join them at Ronnie's house. Not sure what he was going to say to convince them to take part in the school's play, he tried to come up with something as they walked toward the Welsh's.

Shifting the bag containing the elves suits to his other hand, Virgil knocked on the door. Ben answered and seemed glad to see him. "Howdy, Virgil." He looked down at Jack and Tommy. "What brings you gentlemen here?"

"I'd like to talk to Ronnie, if I might."

"Sure, come on in out of the cold."

Ronnie came running toward them, a small, red metal truck in his hand. "Hi, Uncle Virgil."

"Hey, Ronnie."

Ronnie pointed. "What's in the paper sack?"

"That what I want to talk to you boys about."

Jack and Tommy moved closer.

"That's the elf costumes Miss Potter brought to our house," Jack said.

Virgil nodded. "Yes, and I want to talk to you boys about being in the school's play tonight."

Tommy crossed his arms and scowled. "You gonna make us?"

"No, but I'd like you boys to reconsider."

"Why should we?" Ronnie asked. "She don't like us."

Ben came over and knelt next to Ronnie and put his arm around him. "Your mom told me what happened with Miss Potter. But the sheriff assures me that the matter has been taken care of."

"I don't like her," Ronnie said.

"Me either," Jack agreed. "And she don't like us."

"Yeah," Tommy added. "She's mean."

Virgil took Jack's hand. "Sometimes grown-ups have so much going on in their lives, they lose sight of what's important."

"I don't know what that means," Jack said.

"It means that someone was being mean to her and she didn't know how to handle the problem. It made her worry and become scared. That showed up in the classroom."

Tommy tilted his head. "Are you saying we should forgive her like Jesus does?"

"I'm asking you boys to give her another chance."

"But she don't like us," Ronnie said.

Ben turned Ronnie around to face him. "She does, but she's been real unhappy lately and has taken it out on you boys. She's very sorry."

"That ain't fair," Tommy shot back.

"Not fair or nice. So the decision is up to you boys." Virgil held out the sack. "You can go to the play tonight and enjoy yourselves with your other classmates, or stand on the sidelines and watch."

The three boys looked at each other, the uncertainty distorting their young features. Virgil knew they weren't happy with Miss Potter and he hoped that would change. But he had no intention of forcing them.

Ronnie lowered his head and scuffed his shoes against the floor. "I'd kind of like to be onstage with the other kids."

"Well, Ronnie," Jack said. "It's up to you. If you want to be an elf, we're with you."

After searching his father's face, Ronnie stuck his hands in his pockets and looked at his friends. "I'm game if you are."

"Then we are cause we all stick together," Tommy said.

"Yeah," Jack replied. "If we have to sing, why not be elves, too?"

Virgil handed out the outfits, shook hands with Ben, and took Jack and Tommy home. When did negotiating with kids become so damn hard?

"Do you know what we're supposed to do, Uncle Virgil?" Tommy asked.

Virgil shook his head. "No, but Miss Potter will gladly let you know when we arrive at the school."

"Oh, okay." Tommy put his arm around Jack. "At least we don't have any dumb old lines to "member."

"Yeah, but I ain't crazy about singing."

"That's "cause you sound like a frog with a sore throat."

Jack shoved his friend, and Tommy took off running with Jack right behind him. Virgil laughed as the boys raced home. He was glad for moments like this. Jack laughing, Cora carrying their child, and Virgil relived for now that Jack was safe.

He entered the house to the rich aroma of supper cooking. "That smells delicious."

"It's just stew and cornbread. We have to leave soon for the school's play."

"I managed to talk the boys into dressing up. The rest is up to Miss Potter," he said, holding up his hands. "Those are three tough negotiators."

The sound of Cora's laughter filled the house. "Oh, you're just figuring that out?"

Earl came in with Jack beside him. Both were grinning like clowns in a circus. Virgil looked at them. "What have you two been up to?"

"Nothing," Earl said with a grin. "Just manly stuff. That's all."

Sure, Virgil thought. More like getting a little Christmas shopping done. He knew Earl and Jack had something up their sleeves. He just hadn't had the time to figure out what.

Cora set the food out and they all gathered at the table. The stew was delicious and warmed him inside and out. Virgil glanced at the living room and smiled. The house was decorated so nicely he could hardly wait for his parents to see what a great job Cora had done.

As they later enjoyed a slice of chocolate cake, and Jack ran to put on his elf costume, Earl said, "Arthur and me got a lot of shopping done yesterday." He pointed at Cora. "You ladies are going to be busy wrapping presents tonight."

"I know," Cora whispered. "It's so generous of you and Arthur to give so much to the children."

"We have a small fund in the city budget, but it doesn't cover everything."

She met Virgil's gaze. "Maggie and I plan to go to Arthur's right after the school's play."

"I better get a move on," Earl said, standing up and stretching his legs. "Save me a seat, I'll meet you there." As he stepped near the door, he motioned with his head for Virgil to meet him outside.

Virgil pushed back from the table and stood, walked out on the back porch with Earl while Cora cleared the table. "What do you have cooking?" Virgil asked. "I know you're up to something."

"I figured out what me, and you and Jack got Cora for Christmas."

"Thank God," he said. "I've been trying to come up with something."

Earl ran out the porch door. "Follow me."

Curious, Virgil shivered as he hurried across the street to the house Warren Hayes and Ronnie used to live in. Earl went around to the backyard, moving much faster than Virgil thought possible at the older man's age.

As he turned the corner, Virgil stopped and stared, holding his breath. "What is it?"

Earl flipped off the tarp and revealed a black 1941 De Soto, in mint condition with whitewall tires. Virgil whistled. "Damn, Earl, that's a nice looking car."

"I know, and I bought it at a steal." He held out his hand. "We're splitting the price. You owe me two hundred dollars."

Virgil looked down at Earl's empty palm. "What are you talking about?"

"This is Cora's Christmas present. Me, you and Jack bought it for her. Of course, Jack only had forty-three cents to pitch in. But I think it's only fair we put his name on the present, don't you?"

Virgil scratched the back of his head in confusion and amazement. "You got this car that cheap?"

"Yes, I did. I'm right proud of myself."

"I am too."

"Don't go telling me you ain't got the money, 'cause I know you do."

"It's not that, it's just so big. What will we get her next year?"

"You worry about the gawdawfulest things," Earl said. "Let's just get past tomorrow."

"Okay." Virgil looked the car over, checked the interior and kicked the tires. He looked up at Earl. "Did you drive it?"

"Sure did. Runs like a dream."

"A car." Virgil stepped back, amazed at his neighbor's purchase. He'd never thought of getting Cora a car. Not that she couldn't use one. It was that he always thought they'd do that together. But he had to give it to Earl. That De Soto was a great-looking vehicle at an unbelievable price.

"Virgil, since your old pick-up died a few months back, you don't have anything but that squad car. With the new baby, Cora's gonna need to be able to get around. Not to mention your family is growing."

"You're right," Virgil said, running his hand over the shiny exterior.

"Okay," Earl said, taking him by the arm. "Let's keep it a surprise one more day."

Virgil grinned. He doubted Earl only paid four hundred dollars for that car, but he knew he wouldn't win an argument with the older man, so he just accepted the fact that their neighbor wanted Cora to have a car.

After helping Earl cover the surprise, they made their way back inside the house.

"Where did you two go?" Cora frowned. "Virgil, you didn't even wear a jacket."

"We weren't gone that long."

"Well, it's time we leave for the school."

Earl waved and walked out the back door. Virgil smiled at Cora. Boy, was she ever in for a big surprise.

CHAPTER THIRTEEN

The school play was a theatrical disaster. Jack's voice was not only the loudest, but completely off-key. She and Virgil had to cover their mouths to keep from laughing out loud.

Several angels' wings fell off, the baby Jesus wouldn't lie down in the manger and the elves kept stomping their feet to make the bells on the toes of their felt shoes jingle. Cora loved every minute. From the smiling faces of everyone in the audience, the children had done very well.

Cora and Virgil left the school with the boys in tow. Tomorrow night was the big Christmas Eve tree lighting ceremony at the town square and Cora had to join the other ladies at Arthur's tonight to wrap all the presents that would be handed out to the children.

Jack, Tommy and Ronnie ran ahead of the adults as they made their way to the Welsh's house for coffee and dessert. Cora's heart still went out to Ronnie. She loved him dearly and, while she'd had to give him up to Susan and Ben, seeing him happy and well-loved melted her heart and brought a smile to her face.

Looking up, Cora noticed snow drifted lazily from the sky since the wind had grown still, making the cold not so bad. The beautiful neighborhood homes decorated in traditional Christmas ornaments that lifted her spirits. It reminded her of a picture in a magazine.

There'd been nothing like this during the five years she'd spent behind bars. Locked away from society, things didn't change much. Every day was a grind and one day blended into the next.

Freedom warmed her body and touched her heart. She had everything to be thankful for. And life only got better.

Hooking her arm through Virgil's, Cora smiled. This was the happiest she'd ever been in her life. With Virgil's child growing inside her, Jack happily playing with his friends and nothing terrible pulling Virgil away, contentment settled in around her and had her worry free for the first time in what felt like forever.

Inside the Welch's house, after coats and boots were removed, they entered the formal dining room. Susan had the children at the kitchen table and the adults gathered around the decorative table. Susan served fresh coffee and an assortment of holiday breads.

"The singing was horrible," Susan whispered. "Poor Ronnie sounded like a door with a rusty hinge."

"Well," Briggs chuckled. "That didn't keep him from belting out the songs."

They all laughed. "No," Cora said, "I think it's safe to say our boys may have the worst voices, but they make up for it in enthusiasm."

"Oh, there was plenty of that," Maggie said. "Even as elves they were really overacting."

"It was wonderful," Ben said, reaching for a slice of pumpkin spice cake. "I'm glad everything worked out and Virgil was able to get the boys to be in the play."

"That was no easy task. But it was a lot of fun for everyone," Virgil replied.

Brushing cake crumbs off her expanding tummy, Cora stood and smiled at the hostess. "I'm sorry, but if we don't hurry, we'll be late getting to Arthur's and wrapping those toys. Earl said the house was full."

"We'll go and let you men take care of the children," Susan said. "You also get to make up the excuses for why we left."

Cora gave Virgil a stern look. "And no more cake or cookies for Jack."

After kissing her husband goodbye, Cora and her friends left and walked two blocks to Arthur's beautiful house. Ester met them at the door. "I'm glad you ladies are here. We have a lot of presents to wrap."

Inside the lovely home, the scent of cinnamon and snickerdoodle cookies baking filled the air. In the dining room, toys were stacked in separate piles for each family. Gift wrapping paper and ribbons were piled on the small table with scissors and Scotch Tape. "Oh my goodness, we have our work cut out for us," Cora said.

Helen and Nell were there from the dry cleaners and already surrounded by mounds of toys. "It's wonderful to see you, Cora," Nell called. "We've sure missed you."

Cora hugged both ladies.

"I really miss your chocolate cake," Helen mentioned with a smile. "You need to stop by and surprise us occasionally."

The women laughed.

Arthur came in with a tray of refreshments and placed them on the table. "There's plenty of work here and I don't want you gals passing out from exhaustion on me."

Several hours later, Cora, Susan and Maggie stomped through the snow toward their neighborhood. "Have you done all your shopping?" Maggie asked. "I've been finished for weeks."

"Yes," Cora answered. "I finished today. Now I have to find time to get the presents wrapped."

"Oh," Susan said, "I have to wrap everything right away. Ben goes prowling if I don't. Then come Christmas he knows everything I've bought. Since I caught him red-handed last year trying to unwrap a present before Christmas, I fussed at him so much, he's promised not to do that anymore."

Maggie shook her head. "I'm so glad Ronnie will have a nice holiday. I doubt that boy's ever been given a present."

"He's been absolutely delightful and so full of the Christmas spirit. That's why I was glad Virgil talked them into being in the school's play. Ronnie needed to do that to feel included," Susan said.

"Did Ruth say anything to you, Susan?"

"Yes, she apologized and promised that nothing would interfere with her teaching and being fair to all the students."

Susan turned off to go to her house and Cora and Maggie continued home. Maggie sighed. "I have to say, I'll be glad when all this is over and everything gets back to normal. I have a whole house full of people to feed day after tomorrow."

"Virgil's parents are coming, but that's all we'll have. Earl is spending the day with Arthur."

"Do you have most of your baking done?"

Cora sighed. "I'll be baking most of the day. I hope to get the house cleaned, pies and cakes done, and everything ready before the tree-lighting ceremony tomorrow."

"My family wouldn't miss that for the world. It's so exciting for the children. I think Earl is playing Santa this year."

Cora laughed. "That's too funny. He's been wonderful, but very mysterious. I get the feeling he, Virgil and Jack went in together to buy my Christmas present."

Maggie turned toward her house and waved. "See you tomorrow night."

Cora arrived home to find Virgil had already given Jack a bath and had him tucked into bed.

"It's really easy to get him to jump into the sack these days. I only have to mention Santa Claus and he's under the covers," Virgil said.

"He's bubbling over with excitement. I hope he likes his presents."

"I'm sure he will."

Virgil pulled her into his arms and held her tightly against his chest. His strength surrounded her and gave her a feeling of security she'd never experienced. She loved him so much.

"Tomorrow is a busy day and I'm exhausted from wrapping gifts," Cora said. "I'm ready for bed."

"Me, too," Virgil said as he looked around their home. "You sure did a great job making our house a wonderful place to be. What did Jack say about the stockings hung from the mantel?"

"I'm as thrilled as he is. I've bought several oranges, some ribbon candy and a yo-yo to put in them from Santa. You and I will get mostly fruit."

"Fine with me."

"You still have to decide how you're going to make room for the new baby."

He laughed. "We have plenty of time. Let's just enjoy the holidays for now."

She smiled up at him. "I agree."

CHAPTER FOURTEEN

Virgil got dressed the following day and hurried over to Earl's. They'd come up with a plan to surprise Cora with her new car and he wanted to make sure it went off on schedule.

"I found a big bow, but it ain't big enough to go around the car," Earl said.

"Let's just park it in front of the house and place the bow on top," Virgil suggested. Earl, do you have all your presents wrapped?"

"Yes, everything is in place. I'll bring my stuff over tomorrow morning early," his neighbor said. "I want to see Jack's eyes on Christmas Day."

Virgil's chest filled with love. It amazed him how Jack had found a place in his heart that he'd never thought would be filled. Yes, he was thrilled that Cora was expecting their child, but Jack would always be his oldest son.

Earl and Virgil walked into the warm kitchen and found Jack eating scrambled eggs and Cora at the stove. "You men are going to have to settle for eggs and toast today. I have too much on my table to fuss over breakfast."

Virgil put his arms around her and squeezed. "You sit down and enjoy your coffee. I'll fix breakfast."

"If I'd known that, I'd have eaten at home," Earl complained.

Virgil cracked the eggs in the skillet and glanced over his shoulder. "It's not too late. You can leave anytime."

Earl poured himself a cup of coffee. "Might as well stay now. I'm already here."

"Don't let that keep you."

"Stop fussing," Cora scolded. "It's Christmas. I'll have none of it today."

"That's right," Jack said. "Santa comes tonight."

"Yeah," Earl said, smiling. "It's his big night for sure."

"I can't wait," Jack said, his face beaming. "I hope Santa brings me lots of toys."

Cora patted his tiny hand. "I'm sure you'll be very pleased."

Virgil scraped the eggs onto three plates and took the toast out of the oven. Cora had already put the butter and jam on the table.

They ate quickly since Virgil planned to take Jack and meet up with several citizens to put on the finishing touches needed for the tree-lighting ceremony. Earl would be busy getting the toys Cora and the other ladies wrapped last night from Arthur's home to the courthouse, where they'd later be moved under the tree.

As Cora took out the large bag of flour, he kissed her goodbye and headed out the door. The weather cleared up, it had stopped snowing and felt warmer than yesterday.

Inside the squad car, Virgil made his way downtown and pulled into Buford and Carl's gas station. Archie came out to greet him. "Hey, Sheriff. Whatcha up to today?"

"I have to help with the town square." Virgil looked toward the bay doors. "Your dad here today?"

"Yeah, I'll get him."

Archie dashed into the station and soon Buford and Carl carried out a large trough filled with straw. Virgil stepped from the car and opened his trunk. "Can you get it in there?"

"Sure thing," Buford said. "If not, we'll just carry it 'cause it ain't heavy."

"Best if I can drive it there. You men have enough to do today."

As long as Virgil kept the trunk open, he'd be able to drive the short distance to the town square. "I think I'll make it. Ethan can help me unload it there."

"We're about finished with the other stuff."

"Is everyone clear on who's who?"

"Me, Buford and Ethan are the three wise men," Carl said. "Sara Hopper's baby is Jesus, Ester is Mary and we asked the new hospital administrator, Patrick Maloney, to be Joseph." Carl shrugged. "I figured that'd help him feel a part of the community."

"That's a great idea," Virgil agreed. "This way Arthur, Earl, Reverend Washburn and I can hand out presents."

Buford rubbed his hands. "This should be our best Christmas event yet."

"I'm hoping the same thing." As Virgil folded his body into the car, he asked, "You get the animals?"

"You can count on me, Sheriff," Archie said. "The only problem will be getting old man Bryant's mule to cooperate."

Laughing, Virgil pulled onto Main Street and headed toward the town square, which was a beehive of activity. Jack got out of the car and ran toward Tommy, who was there with his father, Briggs.

"Mornin'," he called out. "You better roll up your sleeves. There's plenty to do."

Virgil joined the other men as they worked to get things set up and organized. All the ornaments had been placed on the big tree, but today the lights and garland would be added along with the manger scene. The plastic Santa and snowmen were removed from the storage room in the back of the courthouse and put on display.

Jack and Tommy carried out oversized candy canes and Earl worked assembling a miniature train that circled the tree. In the middle of the square they created a path for children to gather while they waited for Earl and Arthur to pass out the presents.

After several hours, Virgil shoved back his hat then put his hands on his hips. "This looks really good, doesn't it?"

Ethan moved closer and surveyed the town square. "Better every year."

"At least we're not doing all this in a blizzard."

"Oh, last Christmas was a nightmare. I was afraid we'd have to call off the tree lighting."

"We've never done that before," Virgil said, admiring their hard work. "And this year should go off without a hitch."

"The kids are sure going to be happy. The whole courtroom is filled with presents."

Virgil smiled. "The children will love that."

"Don't forget all the goodies that the ladies are making for the occasion."

"Cora is home baking now. She's really busy. I think Jack and I will go home and help her out. If you need anything, give me a call."

"Will do, boss."

Virgil and Jack arrived home to the rich aroma of pumpkin. "That smells good."

Cora glanced over her shoulder at them and smiled. "I hope so. I know your mother makes the best pumpkin pies, so I just made some bread. I'm not competing with her."

Virgil laughed. "I don't blame you."

"Did you get everything ready for tonight?"

"It's almost there. Jack and I came home to help you. We're going to clean house while you bake."

She clapped her floured hands, sending up a white puff. "Thank you so much. With your parents due tomorrow at noon, I wasn't sure I'd get everything done."

"With our help, you will," Jack said. "I'm going to clean my room."

He darted off, Virgil watching, mystified. "He's never volunteered to do that before."

Cora laughed. "It's Christmas. He's on his best behavior."

He agreed then headed for their bedroom to strip the sheets off the bed. As soon as he had their bedroom in order, Cora called them for lunch.

Earl joined them quickly, but had to get back to town to finish putting the final touches on the big event.

Virgil cleared the table then took out the dusting rag to polish the furniture. He thought about what a wonderful time of year this was. He felt giddy as a school boy when he thought of how happy and surprised Cora would be to get her new car.

After a light dinner that night, they bundled up and headed toward downtown. Pal led the way, running ahead of Jack and Tommy. Briggs and Maggie walked with them. "They are so excited," Maggie said. "This is their time of year."

"I'm so happy for them, but I've spent most of the day preparing for tomorrow."

Virgil put his arm around her shoulder. "Stop fussing so much because my parents are coming. They're not visiting to see how clean the house is or how much food you prepared. We're just celebrating a holiday."

"Virgil's right," Maggie said. "Minnie and Roy are wonderful people. Long as you're good to their son, there's nothing you can do to disappoint them."

"I know," Cora said. "But as a new wife I can't help but want to do my best. This Christmas is extra special and I want everything perfect."

They arrived downtown and Virgil marveled at all the residents attending. Young and old, they came together once a year to enjoy the festive event. Children ran around, sucking on candy canes and grabbing cookies from the small booths set up to serve refreshments.

"My," Cora said. "This is beautiful."

"Wait until they turn on the lights."

As they jockeyed for a good viewing spot, his parents came up and stood beside them. "I'm glad to see you," Virgil said.

"We've never missed it," his mother replied.

"And we don't intend to," his father added. "Where's Jack?"

Virgil pointed. "Over there, next to Tommy Cox."

"Now I see him. Those boys are sure having fun. Just look at them jumping up and down."

The crowd quieted and suddenly Judge Garner stepped onto the stage, flipped a switch and all the lights on the tall tree came on. Everyone cheered as the town square came alive. In gestures of good will, everyone shook hands and shared hugs. Before too long, Arthur led the citizens in singing "Silent Night", "Here Comes Santa Claus", and "I'll be Home for Christmas".

The last song reminded Virgil of all the holidays he'd spent in foxholes being fired at by the enemy.

"What a wonderful time of the year," his mother said. "I miss James and Sam most during the holidays."

A pain sliced Virgil's heart like a dull knife. "I know. I feel the same way."

Swallowing a lump in his throat, Virgil felt that sorrow for all those who'd sacrificed so that a little town in Missouri named Gibbs City could celebrate in freedom. All those men who'd traveled to foreign lands and never made their way back home. That was the pain Virgil lived with every day.

Virgil looked across the crowd and on the other side of the street Reverend Washburn approached Miss Potter in a friendly embrace. As he glanced down at Cora and Jack, Virgil hoped Daniel and Ruth might work things out so their daughter would have two parents and they'd become a family.

As the crowd cheered, Santa made a grand entrance, waving to all the children. Jack grabbed Ronnie's hand and ran with Tommy right behind them. They were at the head of the line to receive a present.

"Could those boys be having anymore fun?" Cora asked. "Tonight we'll have a hard time getting Jack to sleep."

"Oh, it only comes once a year." Virgil glanced at Santa. "Earl is having as much fun as the kids."

"He's such a gentle soul."

"He's a cantankerous old man."

She smiled up at him. "But you love him as much as Jack and I do."

Virgil's chest tightened as he gazed across the crowd. "Yeah, I guess you're right."

CHAPTER FIFTEEN

Jack woke Cora and Virgil up early on Christmas morning. They'd made him promise not to peek under the tree until they were all awake. While she and Virgil dressed quickly, Jack ran Pal outside to go to the bathroom.

Earl's voice traveled into their bedroom and Virgil smiled at her as he bent down and kissed her soundly on the mouth. "Merry Christmas, Mrs. Carter."

"Same to you, Mr. Carter."

Holding hands, they went into the living room. Presents were crowded under the tree and a shiny red bike stood propped in the middle of the floor.

"Oh wow, look at that," Jack screamed. "A bike." He turned back to them. "I got a bike for Christmas."

Pal barked and Cora laughed. "You're a lucky little boy."

"Can I ride it?"

"After we open the other presents," Virgil said.

Cora went into the kitchen and put on a pot of coffee then returned as Jack opened several other presents they'd purchased. Earl had insisted on the bike. She wanted to wait another year, but when Maggie said they were getting Tommy the same thing for Christmas, she'd finally agreed.

She gave Virgil the watch she'd bought for him and he seemed very happy to put away the older one he wore in his pocket. Slipping the band on his left wrist, he kissed her and commented that he wouldn't be late anymore.

Vigil smiled when he opened the fishing rod and reel Earl had bought for him. He had to blink back a tear when Jack handed him a small harmonica. "I bought that with my own money."

"I'm very proud of you, son. Maybe we can play a tune together."

Earl kept looking at the large gift wrapped in paper decorated with snowflakes. A big tag with his name scrawled in crayon hung from a crooked bow.

"That's for you, Uncle Earl."

Their neighbor put his arm around Jack and said, "Don't you think you'd be better off calling me Grandpa Earl?"

Jack thought about that for a few minutes then smiled. "I'd like that."

As Earl approached the present, he hesitated. "Now I hope you didn't go spending a lot of money. You have a family to think of."

"Accept the present and be grateful," Virgil said. "You're part of our family, too."

Earl removed the paper to expose a beautiful Victrola. Its glossy exterior, with knobs and fine net screening over the speakers, had the older man stepping back. "My, now what is this?"

"It's a Victrola, Grandpa Earl. It's so you can listen to music."

"Well, I got me a radio for that."

"Now," Virgil said, "you can listen to whatever you want."

Jack handed Earl a flat present wrapped in several sheets of holiday paper and half a roll of tape. A red bow hung in shreds. "Here, open this. Sorry about the bow, but Pal kinda chewed on it before I could take it away from him."

Earl ripped off the paper and held the large record album in his hand. "Hum, Glen Miller."

"I bought you that, Grandpa Earl. Santa didn't bring it."

Earl ruffled Jack's hair and smiled. "Well, ain't that something."

Virgil pushed up from the floor and plugged in the present he'd put together the night before. After Earl removed the paper from the record, Virgil put it on and placed the arm in the grooves. Soon, big band music filled the house.

"That's the best present I've ever got," Earl said, batting back tears. "I know it cost too much money."

"We hope it gives you years of pleasure," Cora said then placed a kiss on his cheek. "Seeing you happy, makes us feel the same way."

Earl cleared his throat and nodded to Virgil.

"Cora," Virgil said. "Earl, Jack and I went in and bought you a Christmas present."

She couldn't imagine what he was talking about considering there were no more presents beneath the tree. "Where is it?"

Jack moved across the room and opened the door. They all followed. Parked in front of the house, where Virgil's squad car usually sat, was a black, shiny De Soto with a big red bow on the top.

"Merry Christmas," they shouted.

She nearly lost her breath. It was beautiful. And as she stepped onto the porch, she realized this wasn't a cheap used car. It was the nicest thing anyone had ever done for her.

She turned and looked at the three most important people in her life and pulled them in close for a tight hug. Tears coursed down her cheeks. "This is wonderful. You are all so kind to me."

Earl swiped at a few tears of his own, and Virgil had a hard time talking. Jack saved them all by running down to the street and opening the door. "Come on, Mom. Take us all for a ride."

She laughed and reached inside and grabbed her and Jack's coats. "Let's go," she called out as Virgil and Earl made their way down the stairs.

Behind the wheel, she fired up the engine and grinned over at Virgil sitting in the passenger seat. Checking the rearview mirror, she asked, "Everyone ready?"

"Yeah," Jack shouted, with Pal on his lap. "Let's see how she rides."

The rest of the day moved swiftly. It wasn't long before Virgil's parents were saying goodbye with their arms loaded with presents and leftovers. Just as they were about to relax, someone knocked. Cora glanced at Virgil. "We have the busiest door in town."

Virgil stood to open the door. "Wonder who it could be on Christmas Day?"

She followed him and as she stepped closer, she saw Naomi and Franklin standing on the porch. "My goodness, you two. Please come in."

Naomi held her purse in front of her and as they stepped inside, Franklin removed his hat. "We just came by to thank you, Miss Cora."

Cora smiled. Her heart lightened at the contented looks on the loyal helpers she'd known all her life. "You're welcome."

"What's going on?" Virgil asked.

"Miss Cora bought us a small house right here in Gibbs City. I can live close to most of my family now."

Franklin ducked his head. "That was mighty generous of you. We never owned nothing in our lives."

"I hope you have years of enjoyment in your own home." Cora moved aside. "Come in and have some dessert. We have plenty."

"No, Franklin's brother and sister-in-law are waiting for us. We spent most of the day moving in and getting settled. The whole community helped with furniture, food and even a small Christmas tree."

"We sure do appreciate the extra money you gave us," Franklin said. "We weren't happy living off her sister."

"I'm glad for you. Merry Christmas," Cora said.

As they shook hands with Virgil and hugged Jack, Naomi reached over and pulled her into a tight grip. "I love you, child. I always have and always will."

Returned the warm embrace, Cora said, "You were my only family when I was a child. I'll never forget that, or what you did for Jack and me when I was first released from prison."

Waving goodbye, Virgil glanced at her. "So, that's what you wanted to use Jack's inheritance for."

"Yes."

"I completely approve, and I'm sure Jack would too."

"They are my family."

"Good," he said, kissing her lightly on the forehead. "Everyone needs family."

At the end of the day Cora felt so blessed she feared her heart would burst with joy. As she cleaned up the kitchen, Jack pulled the front room curtain aside and said, "Look at the big snowflakes."

Cora wiped her hands and joined Jack. The flakes were indeed huge. Stepping out on the porch, Virgil joined them to watch the snow fall from the sky. As long as she lived, Cora would never forget the happiness today brought to her heart.

She was at peace, Jack was healthy and strong and the future stretched out before them. Virgil had moved Earl's Victrola to his house and she'd sent him a plate for a late dinner.

Taking Jack's hand, she smiled down at him. "Are you happy?"

"I sure am." He stared across the street. "Who's that lady standing over there?"

Cora looked but saw nothing. "What lady?"

Jack pointed. "The lady with the light hair in a white dress."

Cora looked closer. A smiling face returned her glance.

Eleanor.

For a moment, Cora couldn't move. The faint image of her sister standing across the street filled her with happiness and love. The presence waved then slowly evaporated.

"Where did she go?" Jack asked.

"To a peaceful place."

"She sure was pretty."

"That was your guardian angel, Jack. She'll always be there for you."

Jack looked surprised then a slow smile moved across his lips as his eyes lit up. "Really?" He turned back to the spot they'd seen Eleanor. "That was my real mom, wasn't it?"

"Yes."

She squeezed him tightly and he went back inside. Cora hugged herself and continued to stare at where her sister once stood.

Virgil put his arm around her. "Are you okay?"

"I am now. Eleanor just let me know I'm doing a good job."

"I've known that from the moment I met you," her husband said, cupping her face in his hands. I love all my Christmas presents, but you, my love, are the most cherished thing I've ever had. Merry Christmas."

ABOUT THE AUTHOR

As long as she could remember, Geri Foster has been a lover of the written word. After raising her family and saying good-bye to the corporate world, she tried her hand at writing.

To her surprise she won several contests, hooked up with a great critique group and her writing career was well on its way. She spent several years studying her craft and developing her voice.

Action, intrigue, danger and sultry romance drew her like a magnet. That's why she had no choice but to write Action-Romance Suspense. While she reads everything under the sun, she's always drawn to guns, bombs and fighting men. Secrecy and suspense move her to write edgy stories about daring and honorable heroes who manage against all odds to end up with their one true love.

53407103R00046

Made in the USA
Charleston, SC
10 March 2016